THE GRAVEST OF MISFORTUNES

ELLA CORNISH

This is a work of fiction. Any names or characters, businesses or places, events or incidents, are fictitious. Any resemblance to actual persons, living or dead, or actual events is purely coincidental.

Copyright © 2021 by Ella Cornish

All rights reserved.

No part of this book may be reproduced in any form or by any electronic or mechanical means, including information storage and retrieval systems, without written permission from the author, except for the use of brief quotations in a book review.

Email: ellacornishauthor@gmail.com

CHAPTER 1

THE BEGINNING OF THE END

On a hot July day in 1862, the Brahampuri village district, situated in the city of Jaipur, sweltered. In the Rajputana Agency, Matthew and Faith Blythe were coming to the realisation that they would never again be happy.

Jaipur was the fastest-growing city in India, and it was a dense chaos with the cacophony and hum of streets, houses, palaces and hospitals rising from the bedrock. Consequently, the city was thick with British engineers, similar to Matthew Blythe, as well as labourer's, soldiers, mercenaries, adventurers, black market racketeers, and, as the unfortunate parents had come to discover, child snatchers.

Bethany Blythe, Matthew and Faith's eighteen-month-old daughter, had been missing for two whole weeks, and it was becoming clear that, maybe, she was never coming home.

The Blythes lived in a walled complex of four opulent stone dwellings which shared a marble terrace and hanging garden with their equally wealthy British neighbours. Matthew's business partner and confidante, Ripley Standish, was one of their neighbours. It was Ripley who had unintentionally crossed the line from hope to despair with what he'd intended as comforting commentary.

Ripley, Matthew, and Faith were in the Blythe's pink marble salon. Faith, as had become her practice in the past two weeks, was standing at the broad balcony doorway which afforded a view over the bustling neighbourhood. She had once been a handsome woman—tall, slim and patrician, with long blonde hair that she normally kept elaborately woven about her—but she had never taken to India and in the two years she had lived there she had only ever smiled for her daughter. Now, as she surveyed the crowds, she was straggle-haired and stony-faced as she clenched to her chest the tepid whisky-and-water that Ripley had handed her an hour previously.

Matthew was of a similar pedigree to his wife. He was tall and of contrasting alabaster skin and rich dark hair. He had developed a practice of squinting against the Asian sun in the manner of a cynical seafaring adventurer. That squint had devolved in the preceding two weeks into a sort of anguished glare.

Ripley looked like the sort best suited to an outdoor adventure or drawing blood on the field of battle. He was broad-shouldered and flat-faced—his usual, impish, crooked countenance was at that moment an awkward dial of discomfiture and worry. His Etonian instincts told him that, of course, this was the moment when a friend steps up and takes responsibility, contriving to engender an air of calm, hope, and the certitude that must surely be the birth right of every born Englishman. Ripley was a clever man, and his schooling had been impeccable—but for this, he had no talent.

"They'll be terrified of the police, I can tell you that much," said Ripley, referring to the Imperial Police which had been formalised by the Government of India Act only a few years prior and had subsequently become a force of terrifying utility in maintaining British exceptionalism. Doubtless, Ripley was right—the kidnappers would be cognisant of the risk posed to them by the forces of law and order and subjugation, but it was not the right thing to say at that moment.

Bethany had gone missing on the 2nd of July. Stolen, it would appear, from her nursery during a crackling great monsoon that rattled the windows and whistled through the rooftops. In her cot was a carefully composed ransom note, demanding twenty-five thousand rupees. This was a king's ransom but well within the resources of the Blythe's, and probably calculated to be so. The following day, another note had been delivered. This one made no mention of the kidnapping nor the ransom, specifically, but merely said that the following day another courier would appear at exactly noon to retrieve the payment. Since then, there had been no further communication.

Now, it was the 17th of July, and Ripley had just said aloud what everyone was thinking. The kidnappers, out of fear of the police, had changed their mind about ever returning Bethany. He had meant it as conjecture, as an explanation of the delay in collecting the ransom money, but the true gravity of the observation was clear before Ripley had finished speaking.

Faith turned slowly toward the men. Her face was an unnerving veil of calm, as though she had found panacea in resignation. She fixed a sardonic half-smile on her husband and said, "India." Then she allowed the glass to fall from her hands. It exploded on the marble floor as if it were a small whisky bomb with crystal shrapnel.

Faith walked slowly and deliberately out the door.

Matthew swallowed his drink in a single throw, strode to the sideboard and the drinks tray, and refilled his glass, not bothering to add water to his whisky. He drank that, too, and then looked at his old friend.

"I believe this is the end, Rip."

"Of course, it's not, Matt," said Ripley, without conviction. "I'm sorry about what I said, but in the worst of interpretations, old man, life goes on."

"I suppose it must," said Matthew.

"I mean, you'll have another child. This is all quite diabolical, of course, but it's not the end."

Matthew reproduced his wife's sardonic half-smile. "You know that Faith never wanted to come here. You must have noticed that she was always quietly resentful."

"It's asking a lot… the climate, the way of life. Any woman would…"

"She's not always so quiet," interrupted Matthew. "We won't be having any more children."

"I'm sorry Matt. I wish…"

"What, Rip? That we could trade places? No, you don't. This is worse. This is a thousand times worse. And at least you were able to bury your wife and, I hasten to remind you, you still have a son."

Ripley, finally, seized on the better part of valour and stood silent as the whisky spoke for his old friend. He listened stoically and heroically as Matthew Blythe compared their fortunes, observing that a widower with a son has a future that a childless man who inspires hatred in his wife can only envy. The whisky burned in Matthew's cheeks and it slurred his words. The sky darkened. Matthew prattled on and then, mid-sentence, he fell silent. He set his glass carefully on the sideboard, and he shuffled from the room.

THE GRAVEST OF MISFORTUNES

∽

Ripley let himself out and stopped on the marble terrace by the fountain, a colourful basin depicting the life of Jai Singh II. The night was unusually clear, for monsoon season, and a big, white moon rippled in the fountain and reflected off the pink marble floor. The sky was a midnight blue from which the imposing Amber Palace cut a black silhouette in the north. Peering over the wall to the south was the pink face of the impossibly ornate Hawa Mahal.

The houses around the courtyard were dark and silent, as though observing this milestone, this evening when everything changed. The heavy wooden gates were closed and chained but they were largely ornamental. A clever burglar, particularly the acrobatic sneak-thieves common to the city, could easily slip through the gap between the double doors. Or they might have scaled the wall or simply walked into the compound during the day and hidden until nightfall. Maybe they didn't take Bethany at all—maybe they'd buried her in the garden as part of some fiendish and ultimately doomed plot to extort the Blythe's.

However it had started, it had ended tonight. Ripley looked back at the Blythe's house, somehow darker than the others, and he knew that Matthew had been right—Ripley wouldn't trade places with him for anything.

"Any news, Mr Standish?"

Handyman Sweet, the usually bubbly Cockney odd-job man to the British business class in the Brahampuri quarter, was waiting in Ripley's drawing-room, entertaining Brother Uckeridge. Handyman Sweet was short and round and balding, and his cherubic, rosy features always appeared cheerful, even now, beneath a knotted brow and glistening eyes.

"Should I go to them?" asked Brother Uckeridge in a tone which belied a desire to do anything of the sort. He was the missionary who converted the generosity of Ripley and his kind into ministrations to the native population. However, the monk was ill-suited to missionary work in India and, indeed, would have been ill-suited to missionary work in Glasgow. He was a thin, feverish man of an indeterminate age between twenty-five and fifty-five, with wispy hair and a frenetic, fragile manner.

"Perhaps tomorrow," said Ripley. "No, there's been no news, but I fear that in itself has been received as a significant development."

The two visitors looked at each other to confirm their interpretation of this. Then they turned their attention to the floor or the twiddling of fingers.

"How's the boy?" asked Ripley.

"Sleeping." Handyman Sweet's spirits rose to the response. "We played in the garden—he can very nearly climb the mango tree—we did a puzzle and then he pretended to fall asleep, so I'd carry him to bed."

Ripley bade his guests good night and stole quietly up the stairs. He peered silently through the door of his son's room and listened to the soft, contented breaths in the heavy, humid air.

∼

THE SPECIFICS of the decay of a marriage and a friendship are too numerous and too subtle to narrate. Faith isolated herself in the bottom back half of the house, where no sunlight ever shone. Matthew ceased contributing to the various enterprises he and Ripley operated together. Ripley tried to juggle the minutiae of infrastructure development and marble-quarrying but was soon overwhelmed. His had been the business end of things—finance and contracts and diplomatic overtures to the grandees of the municipality. Ripley had no head for engineering nor mining, and he found even that for which he had a talent was losing its charm without his friend to admire and appreciate his innovations.

Years earlier, Ripley had developed a manner of formalising legal arrangements with regional potentates who, despite their wealth and considerable influence, couldn't sign their own names. The practice was based on the recent discovery that finger, hand, and footprints were unique to each person, and Ripley was able to convince the Rajputana courts to agree the precedence that a dab of India ink on a finger, placed on an annotated map, constituted a deed. Ripley evolved the method to accommodate the case of warlords at serious risk of losing a hand in battle—they would sign their contracts with a footprint.

It had been Ripley who had stabilised the legal framework of the various enterprises that he shared with Matthew by the simple measure of inviting local luminaries to join the boards of directors. It was Ripley who travelled to Makrana once a month to have tea with the managers of the quarries and the stonemason guilds. And it was Ripley who had to take the final, fatal decisions when Faith and Matthew Blythe embraced defeat.

∼

From that evening on, Faith and Matthew Blythe did not speak. They didn't receive visitors and the day staff had to seek out Ripley for instruction and pay. It was an evening some three weeks later that Faith appeared in the salon where Matthew was drinking alone in the dark. The last, violent breath of monsoon season lashed the shutters and howled in the streets. Matthew had a full beard and a glass of whisky and he was watching the storm through the slats. Faith was wearing the same dress she'd been wearing when he last saw her.

"I'm going to bed, Matthew," she said.

"Good night." Matthew returned his attention to the storm and took another draw of his whisky.

Faith walked to the sideboard, poured a large snifter of brandy, and went back to the door.

"You know… I can never forgive you."

Matthew nodded absently. "I know."

"Good," said Faith. She disappeared into the darkness. She went downstairs to the back of the house, where she'd been living for three weeks. She put her drink on her nightstand, and then pulled the linen from the bed. She rolled the sheets into tight pipes and used them to line the bottoms of the doors. She extinguished the lights and then opened the gas on each of them to their maximum. She breathed deeply and, compared to every breath she'd drawn for five weeks, happily. Then she sat on her bed, sipped her drink, and waited.

Ripley had to take care of that, too. And when, a month later, Matthew was found on the banks of the Dravyavati River, drowned or poisoned by alcohol, or both, Ripley performed his last duty to his old friend.

Ripley sold Matthew's holdings to select enthusiastic board members and he established a series of trusts for much of his own fortune. He sold Matthew's house and belongings and he arranged with the

Bank of Bengal to patriate the Blythe estate to an executor in London.

The beginning of the end of the Blythe and Standish families' presence in colonial India was when Bethany Blythe was stolen from her cot and never returned. The end—the final, grave misfortune—occurred a little over a year later.

CHAPTER 2

UNFORTUNATE ONE

Stella was given the last name of Mallory by the nuns of the orphanage because, when she arrived, they expected her to die.

The name comes from the French *malloré* for "unfortunate one" and it was often assigned by the sisters to children placed in their care showing signs of consumption or Scarlet Fever. The name Stella was an inspiration of the young novitiate who found the child, tied by the wrist to the door of the chapel, on a particularly starry night. It was the dead of winter, 1863, and the nuns estimated that Stella was about two years old.

She didn't have the malignant cough of Tuberculosis nor did she display the scarlet rash. There may have been hope, in fact, and something to be done beyond fervent prayer had Stella's malady been something any of the nuns had seen before, but this little girl suffered a fever so intense that she perspired in streaming rivulets even as she stood in the snow. Her eyes rolled back in her head and she spoke in an unnervingly adult manner of fantastic beasts. The nuns gave her water and prayer and the surname Mallory, and they waited for her to die, because none of them had ever before seen the symptoms of a malaria relapse.

Stella didn't die, but by then she'd earned the name *malloré*, and she'd go on to earn it in even greater measure.

∼

THE CLERKENWELL WORKING Orphanage was convenient to the Clerkenwell Prison and they shared a chapel. The children, aged from infancy to twelve years old for girls and eleven for boys, attended services between six o'clock and eight o'clock on Sunday mornings, and the prisoners would seek forgiveness between ten and noon. While the prisoners, mostly on remand for offences ranging from robbery to murder, were moved between the prison and the chapel, the nuns would lock the doors of the orphanage and confine everyone—including the sisters—to their dormitories. Just before ten o'clock on Sundays, or any other time when the gates of the prison needed to be opened, a bell would peel in the watchtower—once when the doors were opened, and twice to indicate that they had been closed. The guards always rang the bell to warn the sisters that the gates were opening but, except for Sundays, they would usually forget to ring it twice to announce that they were closed.

Both buildings were constructed of brick and granite in the Victorian style, and they had low ceilings and close walls with sunless corridors. On warm days the air in the orphanage was dusty and on wet days the ceiling leaked all the way to the basement. The dormitories were on the main floor, at the end of the hall, around the corner—boys on the left and girls on the right.

The prison had an exercise yard. The children, instead, had working looms, a commercial laundry, and a factory kitchen. By the time the children were four years old, their futures had been determined, largely by chance, and they received training in one of the three professions plus, for the boys, stable work and smithing. For all of the children, the day started at sunrise, when they went straight to work. In the loom hall, they would operate, or learn how to operate, the machines. In the kitchen, they would stoke the stove or shovel coal or fill pies or mix puddings intended for sale in public houses or markets, or they'd prepare the porridge which constituted almost every meal in the orphanage. The tasks in the stable were divided by age or strength. Very young boys filled water pails and cleaned brushes and tools; from eight years old a boy was usually strong enough to shovel muck—from ten he was tall enough to brush, shoe, saddle, and bridle customers' horses.

The day paused for lunch, taken in the kitchen, and then renewed apace with slave labour disguised as learning. The day would end when the work was done, typically around eight or nine o'clock, when porridge would be reheated and served in the kitchen. Evening prayers followed, then whatever ablutions time permitted, finishing off by retiring to a cold, grimy, narrow and thinly covered bed. On Saturday mornings and Sunday afternoons the children would be taught the rudiments of reading, writing and basic mathematics.

~

Stella was deft and a quick learner, and one day, when she was eight years old, she was unceremoniously removed from the loud, frenetic loom hall and taken to the room of whirring, whistling, spinning sewing machines. She was going to be trained as a seamstress.

"Where were you today, Stella?"

This was whispered through the darkness of the dormitory, at the end of that same day.

"The sewing room," Stella whispered back to Mathilda Corbit, who had been her friend and dormitory confidante for as long as she could remember. "I'm going to be a seamstress."

Mathilda choked down a sob in the darkness. There was a volume of conversation and cries that would pass unnoticed in the night, but the children had never tested its limits.

"Stella, you can't be a seamstress. What about me?"

"You can be a seamstress too," suggested Stella. "It's so much nicer in the sewing room, Matty. It's quiet, except for the sewing machines, and they make an ever so jolly sound, like little trains."

"How do I become a seamstress?"

Stella opened her mouth to answer—she was used to having a ready answer to most questions—and then closed it.

"I think they decide," she said at last. "They", of course, meant the nuns, and the manner and degree of control the sisters had over the lives of their charges was, for the orphans, an all-encompassing mystery.

"Can you ask them to decide?"

"They won't listen to me, Matty. Matron Healey makes all the decisions, and she doesn't talk to the children, you know that."

Matty sighed in the darkness and then breathed heavily as she brooded on this.

"*How* does she decide, Stella?"

"I think she must ask God," answered Stella confidently. "Or the Queen."

"The Queen said that you should be a seamstress?" The awe resonated in Matty's voice.

"Are you going to be a seamstress, Stella?" whispered Esmée Trilby from the cot on the opposite side of Stella. At the same instant, the door opened, and a candle flickered in the darkened hall. The girls closed their eyes but otherwise froze in place.

When the door closed again Stella leaned toward Matty and whispered, "Tomorrow, just before the end of the day, tear your smock."

"No."

"You must, Matty. Do you want to be with me in the sewing room?"

"Yes, but I don't want to tear my smock. I'll be beaten."

"You won't. You won't be beaten, and you won't have to be a weaver anymore."

∽

IN THE LIGHT OF DAY, Matty and Stella were very similar, but that was true of most of the girls of the Clerkenwell Working Orphanage. They were slight, even for their age, and they had short, practical hair and white, practical smocks. Matty was freckled and had the upturned nose that people find adorable on children, but only on children, and she had strawberry blonde hair. Stella was clear-featured and of an alabaster complexion, and she had jet-black hair and piercing blue eyes. Her face was of a patrician structure that, on a malnourished child, appeared skeletal.

As the children marched two-by-two from the loom hall, past the laundry and the sewing room, the end of each line grew progressively longer. More boys came from the livery stables and everyone descended the slick steps to the cellar kitchen.

The kitchen served as a dining room when it wasn't preparing meals for the prison, a nearby tavern, and the hospital. This conversion was achieved by sitting the children on high stools at the working surfaces, surrounding an enormous black stove which crackled and coughed and spat burning embers into the thick, smoky air. The walls were lined with iron shelves housing sacks of potatoes and great pots of oats, molasses, sugar, flour, jellied meats, and salt.

The children took their places before steaming bowls of porridge. Stella contrived to sit next to Matty.

"Did you do it?" asked Stella. Matty nodded silently, staring straight ahead.

"Show me."

Matty looked carefully about the room, and then beneath the table, she turned her wrist to show her sleeve to Stella.

"That's not torn," said Stella. "That's frayed. You were supposed to tear it."

"I don't want to be beaten, Stella."

Stella nodded. "Okay," she said and patted her friend's wrist. Then she gazed curiously upward and said, "Matty, there's an ember in your hair."

Matty screamed and raised her arms to slap at her hair and Stella held tight to the cotton sleeve, which split neatly up to the elbow. Matty glared wide-eyed at the damage and then began to cry. Sister Breanna, the statuesque, white-clad and flour-powdered nun who ran the kitchen during the day and enforced discipline at mealtime, appeared like a spectre at their shoulders.

"What's this?"

"There was an ember, Sister," explained Stella.

Sister Breanna sniffed. Sniffing was Sister Breanna's way of expressing most things, but in this case, she was expressing begrudging sympathy—flying, burning embers were a constant hazard in the kitchen. Then she sniffed again, this time to express dismay.

"What have you done to your smock, Mathilda?"

Matty, who had been crying, addressed this question by crying more, and at a greater volume.

Stella was compelled to answer on her behalf.

"It's been torn, Sister."

"I can see it's been torn," said Sister Breanna. "Mathilda, this will not do."

"She can fix it, Sister," said Stella. "She's ever so good at sewing, aren't you Matty?"

Matty managed to nod in firm, jerking, lies.

"Then fix it, Matty, and have it done before tomorrow morning, or you can explain to Matron what's so special about Mathilda Corbit that she warrants the expense of a new smock."

The girls ate their porridge in deliberate gulps and then scurried out of the kitchen in the orderly chaos that consumed the few minutes between dinner and evening prayers. But, where the other children turned at the top of the stairs to continue to their rooms, Stella pulled Matty back toward the halls, through the darkness, to the sewing room.

∼

THE REPAIRS to Matty's sleeve were nearly invisible and, as instructed, she showed them to Sister Breanna the following evening. The next day, Matty joined Stella in the sewing room, to begin training for her future as a seamstress.

CHAPTER 3

THE BOY WHO WOULD BE KING

*L*ater that winter, Stella and Matty were returning from chapel. They were side-by-side at the head of the girls' line, following on from the boys' line. Sister Margaret was shooing the children out of the church, and Sister Breanna was directing them to chores and studies at the door of the orphanage, so neither nun saw nor heard the appalling insults that rained down on the children quite suddenly from a window of the prison. The children heard them, though, and they all looked up in speechless, motionless, shock. All but one boy, perhaps a year older than Stella, who had arrived at the orphanage recently. He was round-faced and broad-shouldered, for a boy of nine, with unkempt brown hair and the bedraggled appearance shared by the boys who worked in the stables, even on Sundays. He stood with his hands defiantly on his hips and fixed a glare on the prison window. A laughing face peered back, so aquiline in its features that the nose protruded between the bars and into the wintry air. The boy surveyed the ground in front of him, selected a good-sized rock, held up the other hand as a sort of guide between his throwing arm and the prisoner, and released his missile.

It bounced off the prisoner's nose with a tremendously satisfying 'tok' and the prisoner yelped and disappeared, coinciding exactly with the appearance of Sister Breanna.

"You wicked, wicked child," she said, gripping the boy's shoulder and giving it a vigorous shake. Meanwhile, Stella was following the scene before her with acute curiosity.

"Please, Sister," said Stella. "The boy was just returning the ring."

"The ring? What ring?"

"A golden ring," said Stella. "The man in the prison threw it to us and said to keep it if we would set fire to the church."

"Set fire to the church?" Sister Breanna staggered beneath the blow.

"It's what he said, Sister."

"I see." Sister Breanna loosened her grip on the boy's shoulder and converted it into a sort of congratulatory pat. "You did the right thing, Teddy. Should it occur again, though, you should bring it to the attention of Matron, so that she might inform the prison authorities."

"Yes, Sister," said Teddy, nodding with a sincerity of which Stella made careful note.

Teddy and Stella walked together back to the orphanage.

"You're terribly clever, aren't you?" stated Teddy.

"You're very good at throwing stones."

"I'm good at everything," said Teddy. "What's your name?"

"Stella."

"I'm Teddy. Teddy Tooter."

"Is it a real name?" asked Stella, referring to the distinction between orphans who know their father's names and those who don't.

Teddy shook his head with conviction. "I chose it. The church gave me a common name. Tooter is King Henry's name, you know. Henry Tooter."

"Why did you choose King Henry's name?"

"So that I can be royalty. What's your last name?"

"Mallory."

Teddy shook his head, this time sadly and with his eyes closed.

"That won't do," he said. "There's no kings or queens called Mallory."

They were inside the orphanage now, and expected to go to their rooms, but Stella put a finger to her lips and led Teddy into the darkness of the corridors and into the vast but empty loom hall. She closed the door carefully and then hopped up onto a stool.

"Can you just call yourself whatever you like?" she asked, raising a sceptical eyebrow.

"Of course. You can do anything you want when you're royalty."

"What happened to your real parents?"

"They were killed in the revolution," answered Teddy with an air of calm resignation.

"What revolution?"

"The French Revolution," explained Teddy. "My father was a duck—that's French for duke—but I don't know his last name."

"I thought the French Revolution was a hundred years ago."

Teddy nodded solemnly as though, despite the passage of time, the painful memory of the storming of the Bastille still rankled. "When I was a baby, my parents gave me to a trusted servant, who sneaked me to England and hid me in a monastery. Then he died, so they sent me here, to be safe from the revolutionaries."

"So, you're really French?"

"That's right." Teddy nodded again. "I'm really a French Duck, and I can prove it. The matron has my family book of lore—it's got lots of papers that say who my father is and that he has a castle in Paris. What about you? Where are you from?"

"I'm just English, but my name is French. Mallory means 'the unfortunate one.'"

"You should change it."

"I like it," said Stella. "I don't want to be lucky."

Teddy opened his eyes wide. "Why not?"

"Someday I'm going to be rich, and it's not going to be because I was lucky, or royalty, or because someone took pity on me. Bad luck makes you smarter. It makes you know what you want."

Teddy looked into the darkness and brooded on this. "You are pretty smart."

"That's because I'm unlucky. And you're good at throwing things. Teddy, are you hungry?"

"All the time."

"Wouldn't you like to get into the kitchen between meals, and get a handful of sugar or a slice of bread?"

"Of course."

"Me too."

The familiar prison bell rang, and the children heard the clatter of the doors as the orphanage was locked down against the sight of prisoners seeking the guidance of the Lord. Stella and Teddy left the loom room and closed the door.

"Meet me at the doors after lunchtime," said Stella, and stole back up the hall.

～

FOR A BRIEF PERIOD on Sunday afternoons the children of the Clerkenwell Working Orphanage were neither eating, praying nor working. This allowed the sisters time to "recompose", as they put it, and this was recognised as a vital aspect of the running of an orphanage. It was the period and process during which all that had unravelled or spilt or in any fashion was found wanting of attention during the week could be addressed with a good, hard, quiet, think. The children, consequently, were unsupervised, apart from by their older numbers, and were expected, above all, not to disturb the nuns as they recomposed.

Sister Breanna and Sister Margaret were recomposing in the kitchen over a clay jug of port. The silence was nearly perfect, and the port was most decidedly so. It was not their practice to talk during these moments. Both would have heartily agreed, though they'd never said as much, that it would have been a grievous sin to break the silence.

And so, when it came, the high, sustained peel of a prison bell, struck once and struck hard, stung like a wasp. The sisters winced, shared a withering look, quickly but carefully poured the remains of their glasses back into the clay jug, corked it, wrapped it in oilcloth, and put it back up the chimney. Then they tapped up the damp stairs, out into the courtyard, and called to the children.

Even before the rock had bounced off the prison bell, Teddy had slipped back inside. He and Stella tiptoed down the stairs and waited in the darkness as the boys and girls were sent to their respective dormitories. They listened as the heavy doors were pulled closed and bolted, and they remained silent while the nuns clacked down the hall to their own rooms. Then, quietly and carefully, they went into the kitchen.

AFTER THAT, Sunday afternoons grew comparatively less unpleasant for Stella, Teddy, and, in time, Matty. Indeed, life in general for the three orphans was measurably more agreeable, partially owing to an increased intake of sugar and bread and, on one memorable Maundy Thursday, some clotted cream, but also due to the camaraderie engendered by secret conspiracy.

Matty needed considerable help in keeping up with her work as a seamstress and failing to do so could soon see her back in the looming hall. The plan that Stella worked out was deceptively simple and closer to a magician's trick than an actual solution. Teddy volunteered to take charge of the stable boys' laundry, which was plentiful and persistent. Attendant with this responsibility was the duty to examine the shirts, trousers and aprons for damage and present them to the girls in the sewing room for repair. Teddy's additional job, as assigned by Stella, was to add one perfectly undamaged article of clothing for every piece that required repairs. Stella and Matty divided up the work, and by the end of any given day their productivity appeared to be very nearly miraculous.

Schemes and connivance require conference and consensus, and the plan that Stella put in place to accomplish this was, in itself, another clever contrivance. Free time isn't so much at a premium in a working orphanage as it is a forbidden commodity, like contraband. The children could speak, quietly and furtively, when the nuns were recomposing, but that was only for a few minutes on Sundays. When a full meeting of the board was required, it would begin with Stella lingering in the dormitory after the workday had begun. Teddy would present the compliments of the stable master to Sister Margaret in the sewing room and explain that Stella had been asked to assist in repairing the saddle of a valued customer, and she was in need of Matty's assistance. Thusly excused, Matty would present the compliments of Sister Margaret to the stable master, and explain that Teddy, owing to his uniquely average build, was required in the sewing room as a living model, to be measured for a dozen pairs of new trousers for the orphan boys, aged nine through eleven. The stable master wasn't allowed into the orphanage, and the nuns never ventured to the stables, and so the twain would never meet.

～

"I CAN'T RING the bell anymore," reported Teddy from the shadows of the stairs to the attic, which was the safest and most distant place to meet during the working day.

"Why not?" asked Stella.

"Sammy Spooner." Teddy said the name as though announcing the death by misadventure of someone who had it coming. "He was caught throwing rocks at the bell. He saw me do it and thought it a topping lark. But he's clumsy as a cross-eyed lamp-lighter—he missed the mark every time."

"Then how did he get caught?"

"He missed the bell, but he hit a guard, right on the ear. The prison complained to Matron."

"Oh, no."

"They sent him to the Soap Pit."

"The soap pit?" asked Matty. "What soap pit?"

"It means he's going to the mines in Sheffield," explained Teddy.

"Soap comes from mines?"

"They just call it that," said Teddy. "It's a coal mine. It's where they send boys who can't do anything else. They send them down the mines while they're still small, and they never get any bigger, because there's not enough room to grow up."

"If they catch you, Teddy, will they send you down the mines?"

"Of course not," said Teddy. "It's only for boys who aren't good at anything. I'm good at everything."

"We'd better be careful, anyway," said Stella. "We'll have to find another way to get into the kitchen."

"Maybe we should just stay out of the kitchen," suggested Matty. Stella and Teddy looked at her as though she'd just proposed that they all join Sammy Spooner in the Soap Pits. "Just for a while."

"I'll think of something," said Stella.

Before Stella would think of a new plan, however, fortune would once again have its say.

CHAPTER 4

MONTAGUE AND CRUIKSHANK

"Stella, remain where you are, please," said Sister Margaret at the end of another long and backbreaking workday. The seamstress girls of the working orphanage had finally completed a complicated series of pinafore nurse's aprons for the hospital, and Stella was warmly anticipating a brief period of standing up straight.

"Yes, Sister," said Stella. "Have I done something wrong, Sister?"

"The matron will be here presently," said Sister Margaret, wilfully distracted by the task of picking stray threads off a neatly folded stack of aprons.

Stella sat in silence until Matron Healey, a hard looking woman composed entirely of grey nun's habit but for a face that appeared to be cast in iron. She walked as though on wheels, expressing herself with a minimum of hand gestures, and her iron face betrayed no emotion. She may have been about to scold Stella or offer her benediction. Stella slid off her stool and stood attentively next to her machine.

"Stella Mallory," said Matron Healey as a statement of plain fact. "I have heard good things about you."

"Thank you, Matron." Stella had never before heard the matron's voice, but it was exactly what she expected—flat and deep and without inflexion, like the sound a drainage pipe makes when you put your ear up to it.

"Stella, tomorrow a very valued contributor to the Clerkenwell Working Orphanage will be paying us a visit. It is the apprenticeship committee of a prestigious clothier, and they will be taking on one girl."

Stella studiously matched the matron's expressionless countenance.

"Have you nothing to say, Stella?" asked Sister Margaret.

THE GRAVEST OF MISFORTUNES

"I understand," said Stella, because she did not, in fact, have anything to say.

"They will scrutinise all the girls in seamstress work," continued Matron Healey, "and then they will select you."

"I don't understand," said Stella.

"They will select you, Stella, because they are already aware of your abilities. The other girls must be given hope, but they're taking only one girl, and it's going to be you. Do you understand?"

"I think so, Matron," said Stella.

"An apprenticeship with Montague and Cruikshank will lead to a very easy life for an orphan girl. You should be very grateful."

"Yes, Matron. Thank you, Matron."

"You must be on your very, very best behaviour tomorrow, Stella," said Matron Healey. "And you must not tell anyone what I've told you, do you understand?"

"Yes, Matron."

Stella brooded over her future at dinner and then at prayer, and she was silent and withdrawn when Matty whispered to her in the darkness.

"Are you cross with me, Stella?" whispered Matty.

"I'm not cross, Matty."

"What are you thinking about?" asked Matty, who knew that this was the only other explanation for Stella's silence.

"Just the future."

Matty lay in silence, blinking at the darkness.

"I don't like thinking about the future, Stella. It scares me."

"You have to think about the future, Matty. I won't always be here for you."

"Don't say that, Stella."

"It's true, though. One day, probably sooner than you think, we'll be too old to stay at the orphanage, then we'll have to find work, and take care of ourselves, alone."

Matty didn't reply, not in words. Stella listened to her friend weeping in the dark.

THE NEXT DAY Stella and Matty were tasked with wrapping the stacks of nurse's aprons in paper and string. Stella folded them like presents and Matty cut the paper and twine in even lengths. Then they carefully shelved the stacks and the supplies, except for the long shears, which Stella placed casually but deliberately on Matty's worktable, next to her sewing machine.

Work was varied and simple—boy's trousers, girl's skirts and nun's habits that needed stitching or patching or repurposing. At some point, the door opened and closed, and Stella sensed that all the girls were being carefully observed. Quiet conversation was exchanged at the back of the room, barely a whisper beneath the mechanical hiss of the sewing machines.

Finally, doubtless out of boredom for a study with a predetermined outcome, the visitors began to walk the narrow aisles between the girls. The apprenticeship committee of Montague and Cruikshank appeared to be formed of a man, who Stella took to be about a hundred years old, and a woman, who she took to be his daughter. They were both very correct. The man wore tails and a top hat, and the woman was in an ornate, pearl-coloured dress made of what might have been silk. The man had a sharply shorn beard and the woman's hair was pulled tightly behind her head, and they both looked ahead with the expression that people hold when reading a book that they don't fully understand.

Montague and Cruikshank walked to the front of the room, turned, and walked back, toward Matty and Stella. In that same instant, Stella's machine made a frightful screech and stopped, drawing everyone's attention. Stella looked aghast at her hands. She had sewn her sleeves together.

"Oh, Matty, help," she said, glancing at the long scissors. Matty leapt from her stool and, with a precise, clean slice, freed Stella from her dilemma.

∾

THE GIRLS CRIED and hugged in the few moments they had the next morning before Matty left to begin her apprenticeship with Montague and Cruikshank. Then, Stella took her place in the sewing room under the judgemental gaze of Sister Margaret. She did little work that day, though, because she was assigned the task of tutoring Matty's replacement, a shy but precocious seven-year-old.

"You wouldn't have liked being an apprentice seamstress anyway," assured Teddy that same evening. He and Stella were lingering on the attic stairs on the pretext of using the livery equipment to sharpen the sewing room scissors. Teddy lay on a bale of straw and Stella sat on another, idly polishing a pair of shearing scissors with an oily rag.

"Why not?"

"They make apprentices do all the worst jobs until they're fifteen years old. You have to wash the floors and sweep the chimneys and muck out the stables."

"We do that here," observed Stella.

"But when you're the apprentice, you're the only one that does it, while everyone else sits around on cushions, and they make you bring them tea and jam and biscuits that they eat while they watch you work, and all you ever get to eat is what they drop on the floor."

"Matron Healey said that it was a good life for an orphan."

Teddy pushed himself up onto his elbows and fixed an inquisitive eye on Stella.

"Did you want to go to Montague and Cruikshank?"

"I guess if I couldn't I'm glad that Matty could."

Teddy lay back on his bale and looked at the night through the slats in the roof of the stable.

"I'd miss you."

"I know you would," said Stella. "Without me, they'd send you to the Soap Pit, for sure."

"Oh, you think so?"

"I'm sure of it," said Stella, with a giggling tease.

"You're probably right," said Teddy, laughing along with her.

"Teddy," said Stella, suddenly consumed by some dark surmise. "You'll be careful to not get sent away, won't you?"

"Don't worry about me, I'll be alright."

"That's just it, Teddy, I do worry about you. I think we should be more careful from now on."

"If you think so. What are you worried about?"

"The mines," said Stella. She leaned forward and looked Teddy in the eye. "You wouldn't be able to grow up if you were in the mines."

"I'll never go down the mines. If they try to send me to the Soap Pits, I'll run away."

"Where would you go?"

"France, probably."

"Do you know how to get to France?"

Teddy fiddled idly with an errant straw. "No," he conceded. "Not really. I used to think that you could get there across London Bridge. The brothers used to make us walk along the embankment every morning at dawn, to a church that I thought was Saint Paul's Cathedral. I would stop at the bridge and look at the other side, and I thought it was France."

"Wasn't it?"

"No," said Teddy, as though the realisation was still a sore spot. "It's just more of London. The bridge never went to France, and we never went to Saint Paul's Cathedral, just a chapel in All Hallows Church."

"I'm sorry, Teddy."

Teddy tossed the bit of straw meaningfully over his shoulder, putting it all behind him. "Doesn't matter. Even after I knew it wasn't France on the other side of the river, I still liked standing there, imagining it was, thinking that one day I could walk over that bridge and go to Paris and live in my father's castle."

"When you go, will you take me, Teddy?"

Teddy caught Stella's eye now with something like reproach. "Of course. What else?"

The certainty that childhood friendships are forever, and that yearning can make something so, only last a short time for the deeply unfortunate, and in a moment Teddy and Stella broke their gaze and cast their eyes downward. Something had changed, today, something sad had become sadder, and something true had become intractable.

They still had each other but, more importantly for Stella, because of her sacrifice, Teddy still had her. It would be several months before that sacrifice would prove to have been in vain.

CHAPTER 5

THE SOAP PIT

In the late summer of 1870 the Bontham Slaughterhouse and Butchers, on Aldgate High Street in Whitechapel, suffered a setback in their experiments with automated meatpacking. It cost the established family concern several days in lost business and it cost one Brian Grady, butcher's apprentice, most of his right hand.

An opening had become available for a butcher's apprentice, so the family patriarch, Jos. Bontham, sent his son, Jos. Jnr, the serious one, to examine potential candidates at the working orphanages of London.

Matron Healey had no frame of reference by which to select boys apt to become good butchers. The closest she could think of to corresponding criteria was that they might have experience with animals, and so she charged the stable master with selecting from his charges the three lads he thought would be most at ease cutting bits off a cow. The stable master had replied that all of his lads were equally good candidates, by which he meant they were each as maladroit and dim-witted as the next.

Forced to choose, nevertheless, he imposed on the boys what would one day be regarded as an advanced problem-solving exercise, asking them, "Which of you boys most hates working in the stable?"

Teddy's was the only hand to go up, but it went up like it was fired from a cannon. The other boys assumed that this was some sort of cruel trick and honesty would only be interpreted as volunteering for some highly disagreeable chore. Most days, they'd have been right.

The stable master chose two other boys randomly and told the three of them to present themselves to Sister Breanna after work, and after they'd cleaned themselves up.

"What's your name, boy?" asked Jos. Jnr. Bontham of the first of the three boys lined up for inspection in the kitchen. Matron Healey and Sister Breanna stood behind the butcher, glaring dire warnings at the boys. Jos. Jnr. was the serious Bontham son, but he often struggled to show it. He was not a tall man, and he had a natural well-fed, bon vivant appearance. He was pink-faced and clean-shaven, and his head was balding and almost perfectly spherical. Consequently, he made a point, when addressing his social inferiors, of lowering his eyebrows and his voice.

"Samuel, sir," replied Samuel Tooley, a gangly and clumsy boy with a nervous disposition and a manner of presenting himself as though he were controlled by invisible strings.

"Samuel what?" prompted Sister Breanna.

"Samuel, sir? Sister, sir?"

"Your family name, Samuel."

"Tooley, Sister."

"What do you know of butchering?" asked Jos. Jnr.

Samuel looked to Sister Breanna for support, but she only raised her eyebrows in a "Well, answer the man" gesture.

"It's done with animals, sir," answered Samuel.

"And?"

Samuel's face betrayed his desperation.

"And… plants, sir?"

Jos. Jnr. moved to the next boy in line.

"Name?"

"Ronnie Padget, sir," said Ronnie. He was the oldest of the three, and he had a shrewd and even diabolical countenance. He had a protruding brow that appeared furtive, as though he was hiding something beneath it, and he emphasised the impression by continuously rubbing his hands together.

"Have you ever seen an animal slaughtered, Ronnie?"

"Just my father, sir."

"Your father?" Jos. Jnr. asked with a gasp.

"Yes, sir."

"Surely you mean that you saw your father wounded in some fashion."

Ronnie shook his head without breaking eye contact.

"No, sir," he said with conviction. "Slaughtered dead, sir, sure as you're standing there. Me mother done it. Used his very own razor, sir." Ronnie accompanied this declaration with a graphic mime, consisting of dragging his thumbnail across his neck, from one ear to the other.

"I… see," said Jos. Jnr.

"Ronnie, you will answer Mister Bontham's questions in a civil manner."

"Yes, Sister. Sorry, Sister," said Ronnie. "She cut him up after, sir, with an axe."

"That's enough," said Matron Healey.

"It's quite all right, Matron," said Jos. Jnr. "Tell me, Ronnie, do you think this experience would prevent you from making a career as a butcher?"

"Oh, no, sir," assured Ronnie. "I likes knives and such. I likes blood and vitals, too."

Jos. Jnr. stepped imperceptibly back and turned to share a meaningful glance with the matron. Then he moved on to Teddy.

"Name?"

"Teddy Tooter, sir."

"How old are you, Teddy?"

"I just turned eleven, sir."

"And what makes you think that you'd make a good butcher, Teddy?"

"Everything, sir."

"I beg your pardon?"

"Everything, sir."

Jos. Jnr. shared another meaningful, happier glance with the nuns.

"That's what I like to hear," he said to Teddy. "Why do you say that?"

"I'm good at everything I do, sir."

"That's just the sort of apprentice we're looking for, a boy of assurance and aptitude. You know, Teddy, I'm visiting several orphanages today, and I'll be meeting a lot of intelligent, apt boys. Tell me, why should I select you?"

"You shouldn't, sir."

"I shouldn't?"

"No, sir, you shouldn't. Not if you care about your business."

"And why not? You just now said that you'd make an excellent butcher."

"Yes, sir. But I don't want to be your apprentice and eat what falls off your table. Even if you choose me, I'll spit in all the meat and I'll burn down the slaughterhouse."

∼

THE FOLLOWING day was a Sunday and so Teddy was able to resort to the emergency meeting call. The boys and the girls were separated on either side of the church with little chance for direct communication. Instead, Teddy and Stella employed a simple system of deliberate error…

As the vicar ended each verse of the litany at which the congregation would dolefully murmur "Good

Lord, deliver us" and "Hear us, good Lord", Teddy innocently reversed the plea to "Deliver us, good Lord" and "Good Lord, hear us". To everyone but Stella, this was an unnoticeable departure from the drone of church services. To Stella, it was a call to arms.

She stopped on the church steps to buckle her shoe and as planned, Teddy tripped over her. Stella pulled Teddy into that tiny, temporary zone of confidentiality between the stream of orphans and the gates of the prison.

"I'm running away," said Teddy. "When I'm rich I'll send for you, and we can get married if you want."

"Why are you running away?"

"They're sending me to the Soap Pit."

"Oh, no. Why?"

"Because the butcher said that because of me he'll never again look to Clerkenwell for apprentices. And he said that he would tell all the other tradesmen that Clerkenwell Working Orphanage is a school for idiots, murderers, and arsalists."

"Arsonists?"

"That's right, arsonists. He meant me. He thought Sammy was the idiot."

"He is, isn't he?"

"Yes, but they're not sending him to the Soap Pit, just me."

Stella crossed her arms and stared into the middle field at some point between Teddy and the prison bell.

"I'll go with you," she said. "We'll go to another orphanage and say that we're brother and sister, and that our parents died in a fire."

Teddy shook his head. "We can't, Stella. I have to wait 'til they send me to the Soap Pit, and then run away."

"Why?"

"Matron has my family book of lore. She'll give it to the pit master when he comes to collect me tomorrow."

"Tomorrow?"

Teddy nodded and again looked guardedly about them. He lowered his voice as he said, "I'm going to sneak it from the pit master. Once I've got my book of lore, I can make a run for it."

"Where does Matron keep it?"

"I don't know," said Teddy. "There's a room, somewhere, where they keep all the treasures of all the orphans. Don't you have any treasures?"

Stella shook her head. "Of course not. How do you even know that your book is there?"

"When the brothers brought me here, they gave the book to Sister Breanna. She got a key from Matron and then went somewhere, and when she came back, she didn't have my book anymore."

"So, if we can find the treasure room, we can get your book and run away before they send you to the Soap Pit."

"Can you think of something, Stella?"

"I already have. This afternoon, you have to ring the bell over the prison gate."

"I will."

"But it has to be before recompose time. That's very important, Teddy."

"I can do it."

"I know, Teddy, but that's the easy part…"

It was the easy part, but it nevertheless required considerable swiftness for Teddy to slip out the front door of the orphanage before the beginning of the nuns' recomposition time. A moment later, the prison bell clanged, and Sisters Breanna and Margaret sighed, called to the children to organise themselves and then march in an orderly fashion to their dormitories, and then they locked the front doors. That part of the procedure went as it always did, but the remaining part, where the nuns confined themselves to their own rooms, was stopped short by a novel and terrifying realisation.

"Is that smoke?" said Sister Breanna.

"It's a kitchen fire," speculated Sister Margaret.

Sister Breanna scrutinised the layer of white mist, roiling about the sisters' hips. It was thick and cumbrous, like river fog, and it smelled of moist wood.

"It most certainly is not a kitchen fire," concluded Sister Breanna. "The orphanage is on fire."

The nuns immediately executed emergency measures. Sister Margaret seized a hand bell from the loom hall and rang it with a violent urgency. She opened the front doors of the orphanage and then she went to the dormitories and ordered the children into the courtyard.

Sister Breanna, meanwhile, sought Matron Healey in her cell, and she, in turn, sent Sister Breanna to the attic with the key to what Teddy had called the treasure room, but was in fact just the key to the attic.

Within minutes, several key events had occurred, some of them were exactly according to Stella's plan, but one of them most decidedly was not.

All the children were safely in the courtyard, and so was a stack of leather and paper billfolds. The nuns would have needed several trips to bring them all down from the attic, but happily Stella had been on hand, and had volunteered to help. Soon enough, the smoke cleared, and the urgency passed as it was realised that there had been no fire, but merely an inexplicable build-up of smoke in the kitchen.

"Somebody deliberately put straw in the stove," announced Matron Healey. Her voice remained unchanged and unemotive, but it was louder and deeper and somehow darkly ominous as she made this announcement to the assemblage in the courtyard. The children stood in four, uniform lines, and each of them focused hard on looking innocent. Matron Healey appeared to roll smoothly between the lines, inspecting each child. She stopped before each of them, leaned forward and, to Stella's growing horror, she sniffed.

"This was a deliberate and wicked act of mischief," she continued, rolling, stopping, and sniffing. "For which the punishment will be very grave indeed." Stella by now knew that she'd overlooked the important aspect of evidence. She and Teddy had lingered in the kitchen, stuffing straw into the oven until the smoke spilt out of it like liquid. She knew that they smelled like a burning building, and she knew that the other children did not. Matron Healey betrayed no sign of awareness or suspicion or anything at all as she tested the air around every single child, and then sent them all to their dormitories to reflect on this villainy, with particular instructions to the guilty parties.

"Don't think you won't be found out," she said. "God sees all."

CHAPTER 6

SIMPLE, WILD, PURBLIND, OR UNGRATEFUL

The fire now smothered, the smoke soon faded and sank to the floor and was absorbed into the walls. The children were allowed to break ranks and return to their dormitories and Stella skipped innocently along with them, but as she reached the orphanage Sister Breanna stepped into the doorway. Her arms were crossed, and she looked down on Stella like Saint Peter, blocking the gates of heaven.

"Matron will speak to you in the chapel."

Stella looked back at the church, small, stone and simple, but in that moment its doors appeared to Stella as grand, ornate gates to hell.

Matron Healey was kneeling before the simple wooden cross when Stella closed the door of the otherwise empty church. There was a cold, mechanical echo, like a bolt driving home into an iron socket, securing the heavy door of a deep dungeon. The nave was dark and only lit by an unnatural blue light of no discernible source.

The matron rose and glided down the aisle to Stella.

"Sit down, child," she said, and Stella sat in a pew. Hope sprang anew, as Matron Healey's demeanour seemed measured and quiet and as close to kindly as Stella had yet to experience from the senior nun.

"Teddy's fate is sealed," continued Matron.

Stella looked down and, for lack of anything else in her line of sight, she focused on a hymn book in a nook on the back of the next pew.

"He will be sent away today," added Matron Healey.

"Today, Matron?" said Stella, looking up. "I thought he was going to the mines tomorrow."

"Is that why you helped him start the fire in the kitchen? Did you think that would prevent him from going away?"

"We didn't start a fire, Matron," said Stella. "There was already a fire, and it was coming out of the stove, so I told Teddy to get some straw, because I thought that would stop it."

The almost imperceptible kindness on Matron Healey's face became truly imperceptible.

"Stella! Do not lie to me, especially not in this holy place."

"Yes, Matron." Stella looked back down at the hymn book. "We put the straw in the stove to make smoke. I saw it once in the stable yard, when the boys were getting rid of old straw. A little bit of fire makes so much smoke that it looks like a big fire when you put straw on it."

"And why ever did you let Teddy persuade you to participate in this wicked, wicked act?"

"He didn't persuade me, Matron, it was my idea."

"Stella, this will do no good. You're lying before the Lord and it will do nothing to help your friend."

"I'm telling the truth, Matron," insisted Stella. She wiped tears from her eyes with her sleeve. "Teddy could never have thought of it. It was all my idea."

"I see," said Matron, in a flat voice that was somehow simultaneously heavy with meaning. She turned back to the cross and looked querulously at it. Stella stole a look at her face, and she knew that Matron was asking God something important. Finally, Matron returned her attention to Stella.

"Stella, you are no longer preparing to be a seamstress. That line of work is for girls who can be trusted, and who know how to appreciate their good fortune."

"Please, Matron…"

"Silence. Indeed, girls who cannot obey the laws of God and this orphanage are not suitable for any future for which we can prepare them. You're ten years old, Stella, old enough to begin work in a scullery."

Stella put her head in her hands. Other girls had graduated from the Clerkenwell Working Orphanage to scullery work. These were girls who were simple or wild or missing an eye, and at ten years old they were deemed beyond hope. To be banished into scullery work meant a life sentence of indentured labour, with no hope nor prospect of achieving anything higher than the lowest domestic servant. The scullery maid, from ten years old until the day she died, was in practice a slave to the kitchen staff, answerable to everyone and equal to none, responsible for the most distasteful and thankless tasks. She would survive on scraps, eat with the dogs, sleep in the coal shed, and be disciplined with a horsewhip.

"Go and prepare your belongings," said Matron Healey, "and present yourself in the main hall immediately. Do not speak to any of the other girls. I will explain what you did, and what lessons can be learned from it."

Stella nodded and then stood. She focused on the ground before her as she shuffled from the church and across the courtyard, under Matron's watchful eye. Sister Breanna stepped aside. Her arms were still crossed, and she looked harsh and authoritative, but the steely condemnation in her eye had become something more like disappointment. In the main hall was Sister Margaret, who had found Stella as a feverish, dying child, tied by the wrist to the door of the church. The young nun clasped her hands together before her face, hiding her tears behind prayer.

Stella studiously resisted the urge to speak to the nuns. She continued down the hall and around the corner toward the dormitories. She passed the girls dormitory, raised her head and her pace, and continued down the hall, through the back passage to the mudding room, and out into the stable yard. She walked with such confidence and deliberation that the stable master said nothing as he watched her unlatch the door in the livery gate. She turned, waved to him, and then stepped out into the street. The stable master, his arms full of uncut bridle straps, looked toward the orphanage, then back at the livery gate. Then he went about his business.

THE CITY WAS a mad clatter unlike anything Stella had ever experienced. The instant of leaving the orphanage and stepping onto the street was more like an explosion than an exit. Hooves clacked and wheels scraped on cobblestones, horses whinnied, and cabbies shouted. Pedestrians and vendors and beggars jostled and murmured in a roar of public dealings and disputes. The streets were deep with horse droppings and mud, and they were enclosed on two sides by cliffs of brick and stone, grimy and greasy with a century of coal. Stella had never felt so small as she stole up the street seeking, in the first instance, calm.

It was late summer, and the evenings were growing cool, but Stella was wearing her smock over a thick woollen dress, tightened at the waist with a leather belt, and her boots were in good condition. She had left the only home she'd ever known, taking with her every possession she'd ever had. She had no food nor money to buy any, but she had something resembling a plan.

It was a clever plan by a clever child, but it was nevertheless the plan of a child. When Stella imagined London outside the gates of the orphanage, she imagined it teeming with nuns and orphans and she expected that on every corner was an orphanage which shared a courtyard with a church and, possibly, a prison. She expected that she would be able to select the most welcoming of a dozen such places—how big could London be, after all—tell her tragic story, and a bed would be found for her. In time, she supposed, she'd have figured out a way to retrieve Teddy from the Soap Pit in Sheffield, which she expected was a few streets north of Clerkenwell.

Stella was driven by visions of table scraps and scullery work, scrubbing pots and unsticking drains of unspeakable clogs for all of her days. She hugged herself against the creeping chill of evening as it fell, and she selected turns and crossings by looking ahead to the next corner—if it was a church or in any way institutional, that's where she went. But the churches were austere and if they weren't closed and locked there was a deacon or policeman to tell her to go do her begging somewhere else. And the institutional-looking buildings were societies or banks or smart residences, with tall iron gates and no space for orphans.

For an hour and a half, Stella had resisted all temptation to cry. Even when the sun was gone and the wind began to blow brisk and cold up the street, she bore down and ahead. When the rain began, though, Stella coughed an involuntary sob. The rain soaked through her smock and then her dress and, as her face was wet anyway, she allowed the tears to come. It was when she ran out of road that Stella finally stood on the riverbank, overwhelmed by the breadth of the Thames, inky and foreboding in the night and roiling in the rain, and wept long, loud wails of despair.

Stella knew that London had a river, but she'd never seen it. In her imagination, it had been more like a creek, with grassy banks and trees and steppingstones. The Thames appeared to her now, with lights blinking in the darkness on the far bank, more like how she'd imagined the English Channel. She knew it wasn't the ocean, though, because oceans don't have bridges, and there to her left, an arching great silhouette against the smoke-grey sky, was London Bridge. On the other side, she knew, was just more London. This is where Teddy had stood and dreamed of his father's castle in France.

Before her was the cold, churning water and behind her were the closed, cloistered mansions of the wealthy. Beneath her feet was mud and lashing down from the skies was a penetrating rain. But there, beneath where the bridge dove away from the bank and into the river, was shelter.

The moment she trusted her weight to the sodden bank it betrayed her, and she slipped into the mud and slid down the incline. It was not how she planned it, but now she was at the entrance to the northern arc of London Bridge, yawning before her like a cave and echoing with the slaps and sloshes of a rushing river. It was dark and damp under the bridge, but it wasn't raining. Shadowy figures paced deliberately along the water's edge. To Stella, it appeared as though they'd lost something and were searching for it intently, but what really mattered was that they weren't looking at her. She pushed herself into the crevice formed of the rocky bank and the bottom of the bridge. She hugged her knees to herself, and she cried. She cried for the sewing room and her bed, and she cried for Sister Margaret. She cried for the orphanage which had never been home, exactly, but it had at least been dry. She cried for Teddy and Matty and she cried because she was hungry and tired and lonely. She cried because crying was all she had left.

CHAPTER 7

THE ALDGATE APPRENTICESHIP

The rain and rocking of the river melded into a whirring drone, faded into a dream, and then returned as the sound of gulls and bargemen. The inky darkness had become a grey, misty morning and though Stella was still cold and wet, her more immediate concern was that someone was stealing her boots.

Instinctively she kicked out. Her boot found solid footing in a yielding face, from which burst a sincere "Woof!" as a boy of about twelve tumbled down the bank.

The boy somersaulted backwards and then landed on his feet. He put his hands on his hips and he fixed Stella with a resentful grimace. He was wiry and jumpy and dressed like a hobo—his trouser legs were different lengths, and his jacket pockets were patches from other garments.

"What did you do that for?" he demanded.

"You were taking my boots," said Stella, pushing herself further into the crevice between the bank and the bridge.

"'Course I was," said the boy cheerfully. "I thought you was dead."

"You steal boots off dead people?"

The boy shook his head energetically. "'Course I don't. Mostly they been in the river for days, they ain't worth the trouble and, believe me, by then, getting boots off a body is plenty of trouble."

Stella's situation was rapidly clarifying. She remembered where she was and how she got there, and she became acutely aware that she ached everywhere and that she was ravenously hungry. She'd left the orphanage before the evening meal and she'd walked for hours. Her clothing was wet, and she was sitting on a wet riverbank, facing off a boy who stole from corpses. And he wasn't alone. The figures that she'd seen last night were still there, pacing the water's edge and looking for something they'd lost, and Stella realised that they were, in fact, looking for things that others had lost. They weren't silhouettes anymore, and they weren't full-grown men, but young boys and girls, much like Stella, although even more ragged and desperate.

Stella was inspired by a new line of enquiry.

"What's your name?"

"Pitt," said the boy. "Pitt Pewter. Call me Pitty."

"I'm Stella." Stella moved out of her defensive nook. "Are you an orphan?"

"'Course," said Pitty.

"Where do you live?"

"In a coach."

"A coach?"

"A coach." Pitty nodded. "It's a dandy, too. A hearse."

"You sleep in a hearse?"

"Better than under a bridge," said Pitty defensively.

"Don't you live in an orphanage?"

"'Course not." Pitty laughed. "Orphanages are for those got nowheres to live."

"I have nowhere to live."

"I can see that." Pitty turned to look up the bank, to where the sun was steaming fog off the river. Then he called out. "Twick!"

An older boy, presumably called Twick, was in conversation with a stout, older man in many layers of clothing. Twick was perhaps fourteen years old but he had about him the demeanour of an older, cynical man. He was dressed like Pitty, although not quite so raggedly, and he wore a woollen cap. Twick and the man concluded some business that involved the exchange of something small for something bigger, and then he wandered over to Pitty and Stella.

"What is it, Pitt?" Twick sounded as though Pitty, despite the early hour, had already tried his patience.

"This is Stella," said Pitty. "She's got nowhere to live."

Twick put his hands on his hips, scrutinised Stella briefly, and then looked back at Pitty.

"So?"

"So, can she come stay with us? She's an orphan, and she's got nowhere to go."

Twick looked back at Stella, who smiled an innocent, helpless, homeless smile.

"Go to an orphanage," said Twick. "It's what they're for."

"I just ran away from an orphanage," said Stella. "They were going to make me take on scullery work."

"It's work ain't it? You're lucky to have it. Scullery work is for those who can't do nothing else. There's lots of girls can't do nothing would be happy to be a scullery maid." Twick turned his attention to the riverbank and started to walk away.

"I'm not a scullery maid." Stella scrambled to her feet and stalked down the bank toward the boys. "I'm not one of those girls who can't do anything." Stella remembered how convincing and intriguing Teddy had made himself. "I'm good at everything I do."

"Oh, yes?" mocked Twick. "What can you do?"

"I'm a seamstress," said Stella. "And I can run a loom, bake a cake, and shoe a horse."

"You know about looms?" Twick raised his head and regarded Stella beneath hooded eyes, as though she'd just said that she knew where to find buried treasure.

"And I'm a seamstress, and..."

"Yes, you said all that, but do you know how to work a loom?"

"I said so."

"Is anyone after you? Is there going to be any trouble if you come with us?"

"No."

"Let's see what you know about looms, then." Twick put dirty fingers to his teeth and blew a short, sharp whistle. Three more children among the scavengers looked up and gathered round. There was another boy, about ten years old, a girl about Stella's age and another about eight years old. They were all grubby and dressed in the torn, poorly patched coats and trousers and dresses of the career street urchin.

The children carried cloth sacks and as they approached Twick they opened them for inspection, and he pronounced judgement.

"Rubbish, rubbish, keep the candle, you never know, rubbish, them spec's might be gold, rubbish… what's that, Lucy?"

The seven-year-old looked into her sack, then back at Twick.

"Seashell," she said. "It's pretty."

"I think it's a bit of broken teacup, Lucy."

"Still pretty."

Twick shrugged. "Scatter everyone. Meet back at the office."

At this announcement, the children scampered off in all directions. Pitty took Lucy by the hand and scrambled up the bank.

"We'll go this way," said Twick, then led Stella to the opposite edge of the bridge.

∼

THE OFFICE, it seemed, was somewhere north of the river. Stella was hopelessly lost and had been since she took the first corner after leaving the orphanage the day before, so she relied entirely on Twick's circuitous navigation, even though Stella suspected that they were covering the same ground twice. Twick spoke as they walked, dispensing the wisdom of his years, and Stella felt that she was learning something that she didn't understand, and it was even somehow related to the inexplicable route that they were walking.

"Stella your real name?"

"I don't know my real name," said Stella.

"I mean, is that the name they gave you at the orphanage?"

"Of course. What else?"

"Never tell no one your real name," said Twick. "And never use the same name twice in a row."

"Why not?"

"And listen, don't let no one ever follow you to the office. You see someone following you, you don't come to the office."

"Why not?"

"A peeler ever asks you where you live, you tell them the orphanage."

At some point, Stella realised that replying why or why not or anything at all was a poor use of her fading strength, and so she walked on and made note of Twick's stream of sage non-sequiturs.

When Stella saw the simple brick and granite structure of Saint Botolph's Without Aldgate her heart leapt. As parish churches go, Saint Botolph's was pleasant and functional, but compared to the little chapel that the Clerkenwell Working Orphanage shared with the prison, it was a cathedral, and Stella's logic dictated that it must be associated with a correspondingly impressive orphanage.

"You live here?" she asked Twick.

"'Course not," he said with disdain. "No one lives here. They're all dead."

And with that Twick stopped at the wooden door in the stone wall of the churchyard, looked both ways, and then pushed it open, leading Stella into a small, enclosed cemetery behind the church. Twick put his fingers to his lips, pushed the door closed, and weaved his way through the gravestones toward a grand mausoleum that looked to Stella like a little stone chapel.

Twick rapped a complicated beat on the door of the little building, and it creaked open.

The interior of the mausoleum maintained the illusion that it was a church, with a crucifix below a single, narrow, stained-glass window that bathed the congregation in red light, and a congregation—children ranging in age from seven to seventeen—that sat on the floor and on the sarcophagi of the antecedents of some wealthy family. In the place of the minister was a tall, thin man of between forty and sixty years, wearing the mismatched parts of seven or eight fine suits. His long hair was tied tightly back, and his greasy beard had been formed, by habit of constant pulling, into a conical horn on his chin.

"Who's this, Twick?" asked the preacher, in an unnerving manner that made Stella think of a glutton asking what's on the menu.

"Stella," answered Twick. "Pitty found her sleeping under London Bridge. Says she's got nowhere to go."

The preacher turned a bemused, judgemental expression on Pitty.

"You believed someone else's pity story, Pitty?"

Pitty shrugged. "She had good boots," he said, and the preacher nodded as though that was a satisfactory explanation.

"Why did you bring her here?" he asked Twick.

"Says she knows how to work a loom."

"Knows how to work a loom, does she?" The preacher stroked his beard, as Stella would soon notice he did constantly, when his hands weren't otherwise occupied. He approached Stella and squatted down to look her in the eye. "Hello Stella. I'm Jacob Nightly, and these are my apprentices. They all have special skills and talents, but none of them can work a loom. Can you?"

"I've said I can."

"So, you have," said the preacher. "But is it true?"

"Yes."

"Then explain it to me."

"I can't," protested Stella. "I can only show you."

Jacob Nightly stood again and smiled down on Stella.

"Words, Stella, are the most powerful thing in the world. Language is what separates us from the beasts and permits us to argue our case before the Lord. With words anything that exists, and most of that which does not, can be made manifest in the mind of man."

"I don't understand."

"Just tell me how a loom works, enough to picture it in my head, not enough to become a weaver."

Stella looked around at the congregation. The children, including Pitty, Lucy and Twick, were gazing at her with wide eyes and focused expressions. She didn't know why or to what degree, but Stella knew that she had something that they wanted.

"I'm hungry," said Stella.

"Story first," countered Jacob.

Stella searched the room from where she stood and spotted a planting pot, upturned to make a stool. She walked to it, sat down, crossed her arms, and faced Jacob.

"I'm hungry."

Jacob squinted at Stella, as though trying to read her mind.

"Rudy, what have we got for breakfast?"

The ten-year-old boy who must have been Rudy was perched on a stone coffin with a burlap sack on his lap. He upturned it onto the granite surface and out spilled a broad assortment of damaged carrots, turnips, apples, cheese, and partial loaves of bread. The congregation gathered round the buffet, but Jacob said, "Stella first," and the children stepped aside.

The restorative powers of raw carrots and turnips are limited, as a rule, but to a nine-year-old who hasn't eaten in a day and who has since slept under a bridge, it was nothing short of a feast.

Consequently, Stella was generous with what she could put into words regarding the working of the looms with which she was familiar. She described, in childlike and, in light of her audience, effective terminology, the difference between a treadle loom and a dobby loom, the duties of the warner and webster, without employing either term, and the draw boy, usually a girl. She explained how to beam and roll the fibres and thread the heddles. It was when Stella described the importance and delicacy of the operation of the shuttle that Jacob said, "Just a moment… say that bit again."

"The shuttle is like a little boat, loaded with yarn, and it crosses between the weave at each pass."

"I see," said Jacob, stroking his beard.

"Lucy, take Stella to the vestibule. Get her some dry clothes and set her by the stove."

Lucy slid down from a sarcophagus and took Stella by the hand.

"Tonight, bring her to the coaches and make sure she gets a comfortable night's sleep," added Jacob.

"Tomorrow, Stella, we're going weaving."

CHAPTER 8

THE IMPORTANCE OF SMALL THINGS

Stella passed an uneventful day in the vestibule of Saint Botolph's church, behind a woollen curtain next to a stove. She dozed and woke and dozed and woke and intermittently listened to Jacob Nightly receive visitors in what turned out to be his place of business. She hadn't noticed, and probably wouldn't have understood, the plaque on the door reading, "Aldgate Apprenticeship, prop. Jacob Nightly, Esq." It was a nicely polished brass plaque and it looked reassuringly fixed to the stone, but this was an illusion that Jacob recreated every morning, and it gave the impression that he operated a charitable organisation, sanctioned by the church. Every night, or whenever there was a risk that a member of the clergy might visit the yard, he popped the plaque off the wall and into his pocket.

It was late that night that Lucy led Stella once again out into the streets of London. It was colder now than it had been the night before, but Stella had dry clothing and the promise of a warm bed. After an hour of circuitous meandering and a distance that could otherwise have been covered in about fifteen minutes, the smell of horse—a universal characteristic of the air in London—grew stronger, and presently the girls arrived at a grand, brick barn with high, arched doorways. Above the centre door —itself the height and width of a small building and painted a shiny black—was a sign reading 'Henry Radcliffe & Sons, Livery to the Trade'.

Lucy tapped a tune on the people-sized door embedded in the stable door—possibly the same rhythm that Twick had rapped to gain entry to the graveyard—and the door was pulled open by a stern-faced boy with an oversized top hat and a finger to his lips.

The courtyard of the livery stable was like a little village, and the houses were cabs and carriages and two long, black hearses. Stella was charmed beyond measure—everyone had their own little home, on four wheels and with springy suspension, walls, roofs, and windows and even curtains. A big white moon lit the village as if it were a fairy kingdom, and in the silence and the fog and the sheer novelty of it all Stella felt transported, as though the Clerkenwell Working Orphanage was a thousand miles away, and her life there a thousand years ago.

Lucy and Stella selected a small but cosy hansom cab with two upholstered benches and blankets for the passengers, and they settled in for the night.

"We must be very quiet," whispered Lucy. "And we have to leave everything just as we found it and be away before sunrise. Willy will knock on the door in the morning, to remind us."

"Who's Willy?" Stella whispered back.

"He's the stable apprentice. Mister Nightly give him to the livery for free, and he watches over the place at night, to make sure no one does nothing to the horses. He lets us in and sees to it we're gone by morning. Sometimes coaches come and go at night, so we have to be very quiet and sleep with our shoes on."

STELLA SLEPT SO SOUNDLY and so deeply that she felt as though she'd gained no rest, as though she'd put her head to the cool leather of the bench and a moment later Willy was tapping on the door of the carriage, reminding them that their day had begun.

As everyone soundlessly quit their fairy village homes Stella counted about a dozen children in total, many of whom hadn't been at the office the day before. Twick was in the street, assigning addresses and tasks to children who would instantly run off in all directions.

"Lucy and Stella, you're coming with me. Pitty, you are too. Annie, Liza, Emma, you as well."

When all the apprentices had been given assignments, Twick led his little team back down to the river and across the bridge and into the labyrinthian streets of industrial Bermondsey, where they sat on a dock and breakfasted on stale bread and waited for sunrise.

"That there is a weaving mill," said Twick, pointing to a brick factory on Chambers Street, like a dozen other brick buildings along the south bank. A newly painted sign on the first floor read 'Bermondsey Weavers'. "They've got a big order to fill, and they want six smart hands, experience not necessary but knowledge of looms desirable. Stella, you just have to make sure all that bit's bang up, right?"

"Bang up?"

"Just work the loom, and see to it that Pitty, Lucy, Annie, Liza, and Emma do too."

The sun rose, the doors of the factory opened, and Stella once again found herself in a vast loom hall. These were all the latest power looms, driven by the force of the river current, but they were functionally identical to the fifty-year-old machines at the orphanage, and before the tasks had been assigned Stella was accounting for herself—and the Aldgate Apprenticeship—with an aplomb which belied her age. Twick effected to supervise, walking from machine to machine and casting a fastidious eye over his charges and giving a very convincing impression of a young man who understood weaving. At the end of a long day, as the sun was setting on the river, Twick offered Stella's services in overseeing the shutdown—replacing the water where necessary, checking for and removing errant threads that can be caught in the works, and rewinding the shuttles for an early start the next day.

THE GRAVEST OF MISFORTUNES

~

THE NEXT DAY was a Wednesday and Samuel Lipton, the floor supervisor of Bermondsey Weavers, was wondering where his apprentices were. His regular workers were arriving, and work would be starting presently, and so he began to make contingency plans. If the apprentices didn't come, two of the eight looms would have to sit idle, and everyone would have to work another two hours tonight and tomorrow. As he stood at the door of his factory and mused on the poor hand the morning had dealt him, a round, jolly figure appeared before him.

"Mister Lipton, sir," said the layered figure. "I am Sweeper."

"You don't say," said Samuel. "We're not looking for casuals, especially not sweepers. Can you work a loom?"

"I cannot, sir, in the traditional sense," said Sweeper, with a tobacco-coloured smile that suggested that this was, nevertheless, good news. "I can, conversely, make a loom work."

"Sell it somewhere else, gigglemug, I'm a busy man."

"I put it to you, sir, that you are not, and will remain so until you and I have concluded our business."

"What business?"

"That business," said Sweeper, gesturing with a glance to the interior of the factory. The weavers were examining their machines, wandering around them and crawling under them or generally standing about looking bewildered.

Samuel finally made the connection between Sweeper and the Aldgate Apprenticeship. He didn't know what that connection was, yet, but he knew that two things were amiss this morning, and that this man somehow connected them. Had Samuel been present the previous Monday morning underneath London Bridge and seen Sweeper making furtive arrangements with Twick, he might have understood the situation more clearly, and he certainly would have understood it more quickly.

"What's happening? What have you done to me looms?"

"Nothing at all, Mister Lipton. So far as I know, they're all in perfect working order. However, I have come into possession of a cache of materials that may allow them to work even better—two dozen shuttles."

"Shuttles?"

"Yes, sir, shuttles," said Sweeper, miming the device with his hands. "They are a sort of boat-shaped contraption, with a spool, for passing…"

"I know what shuttles are, you low-life mace, have you nicked mine?"

"Nicked? How dare you, sir. I have come into possession—pursuant of my honest profession as a restorer of used industrial materials—of a shipment of twenty-four almost new and perfectly serviceable loom shuttles, and I'm prepared to part with them for a very fair price of six shillings."

"Six shillings? For my own shuttles?"

"Each."

"That's more than they cost new."

"You have me at a disadvantage, sir," confessed Sweeper. "This is not my core business. I'll take your word for it. Nevertheless, I have to recover my investment, and I paid five shillings each."

"You never did."

"I have given you the benefit of my credulity, good sir. I would ask you to afford me the same consideration."

"You're a crook."

"And you're running out of time, Mister Lipton. As proof of my good faith, I offer you a sample of my product." Sweeper reached into the many folds of his suits and withdrew a long wooden boat-shaped device, trailing a thread of yarn.

"That's mine."

"For the one-time price of six shillings. Cash only. Once we have reached a satisfactory conclusion, I will bring the other shuttles, one-by-one, for six shillings each. Do we have a deal?"

Samuel cast a grudging eye over his loom hall, which was quiet but for the confused murmurings of his workers. Bales of yarn stood unexploited against the walls. The gears of the water turbines droned beneath the floor, yearning to power some looms. Above all, the day ticked away toward the point when he would have to explain to his employers that he had failed them and that they would be unable to deliver the biggest order that Bermondsey Weavers had yet received.

"Very well," conceded Samuel through gritted teeth. "We have a deal."

∽

THE OBVIOUS DISADVANTAGE of running a dishonest apprenticeship, even in a city the size of London, is the absence of repeat customers. It would be years before Bermondsey Weavers would trust another such service. By then, of course, there would be a new floor manager and the fundamental deniability of what had been done would prevent any accusations from ever seeing a court of law—Bermondsey Weavers had asked for six "apprentices". Of course, what they wanted was six children who would work for next to nothing during a brief surge in demand. They received exactly what they asked for—six hard-working, low-paid children who did what was asked of them and more. The presence of a seventh, obviously dishonest, young man could hardly be blamed on the Aldgate Apprenticeship or its proprietor, and indeed reflected more on the care and caution of Samuel Lipton than it did on anyone else.

Nevertheless, the key to survival in the fake apprenticeship game was constant evolution. Jacob

Nightly moved the offices from the vestibule of Saint Botolph's Without Aldgate to a gardener's shed in Stepney and from there to a boot room at the back of an hotel in Farringdon, and back again to Saint Botolph's. He was constantly presenting the economic advantages of a destitute workforce to new industrial clients, and of course, the apprentices themselves were rotated out as they grew too old to be convincingly exploited.

Above all, it was vital that the game itself was constantly changing. By the time Stella was sixteen she had been with the Aldgate Apprenticeship for six years, and she had contributed to some of the most effective of these new schemes.

"Them's Saint Katherine docks," said Stella, now a young woman standing across the river on Butler's Wharf with Pitty, now seventeen years old. It was a cold autumn evening, and the sky was grey with warning of colder nights to come. "Tomorrow they want some lads to pack and weigh sacks of coal for the big hotels—sixpence for each sack."

"They're paying sixpence just for loading a sack?"

"No, stupid, that's what the guests pay if they want to be warm," said Stella. "The docks're paying aught but the tuppence per boy that Mister Nightly'll keep to himself."

"What's the lay then?"

"There's four bags—the Hotel Grand Arch, Brown's, the Saint James, and Doon's Waterloo. It's you and three other strong lads that you bring along—they'll give you each ten bags at a time. You go to the barge, a coal man shovels you a sack full, you take it to the scales, they weigh it, then you load it on one of four carriages. The bargeman ain't going to shovel you nothing if you don't have the right sack… right size, right name of the hotel, you get it?"

"No."

"It's where being a seamstress pays off, now, isn't it? I made you forty sacks that look just like the real thing. Tomorrow, you each put ten sacks under your coat…" Stella opened Pitty's coat and patted his scrawny rib cage, "…here, and here. Every second sack you fill, it's one of ours, you get it weighed and then, instead of putting it on the cart, you drop it off the dock—Annie and me'll be there in a dory."

"What are we going to do with all that coal?"

"Sell it to Sweeper. He's giving us thruppence a bag."

A cold wind swept off the river and Stella pulled her shawl tighter in a largely token effort to fend off the chill. Pitty stepped close and put his arm over her shoulders.

"What's that then?" asked Stella, regarding Pitty from beneath raised eyebrows.

"Helping you stay warm, is all."

"Get me that coal, Pitty," said Stella, extricating herself from Pitty's embrace. "That's all the warmth I need from you."

CHAPTER 9

A BARGAIN AT TWICE THE PRICE

Cash and coal and the proceeds of extortion are easily enough stored and sold on, but the Aldgate Apprenticeship was an organisation constantly on the move, and over time the need arose to store larger and more conspicuous items. It was Stella who found the barge, and in time she'd think back on that day and wish that it had never happened.

The Limehouse Cut is a canal which, by then, had already been in heavy use by grain merchants to ship merchandise from as far north as Stevenage. It drained into the Thames via the Limehouse Basin, and it was very convenient to the warehouses along the river. The canal went into competition with the railway starting from 1850, inspiring an initiative to widen the Limehouse Cut. The muddy banks and ill-confident backers ensured that the project to add twenty-five feet to the canal's existing fifty-foot width took upwards of twenty years. During that time, traffic on the canal slowed, a few ageing barges fell out of use, and for a while, many of them lay beached along the edges of the occasional dredging site.

Initially, Stella investigated a narrow freighter called *Maltsack* as potential living quarters for the apprenticeship. It was still afloat, and it had an iron stove and ample storage space. The hull, however, was flooded, and it was too dangerous and damp to function as a dormitory, but it was easily accessible from Cable Street and yet hidden beneath a bridge. The bridge, in turn, offered easy access to the towpath, and the canal offered easy access to the Thames, for delivering stolen coal by water.

In time *Maltsack* became a lair, and a hideaway. The apprenticeship tidied up and patched the interior, while deliberately making the exterior look as much like a rotting and valueless hulk as possible. It listed badly into the bank and this effect was exaggerated by ballast in the hull. The effect, from the outside, was a barge that looked as much like a dead body as a barge could, while on the inside the incline raised the damaged part of the hull out of the water far enough to create a large, dry bulkhead. It was used for the temporary storage of everything from coal to corn, and the long-term storage of more valuable treasures not so quickly sold on, including clocks, jewellery, and candlesticks. Jacob began to think of the *Maltsack* as a sort of retirement fund, the liquidation of which would mark the beginning of his life as a gentleman of leisure. Before that, though, the existence of the barge would lead to a minor evolution in the affairs of the Aldgate Apprenticeship and a major turning point in the life of Stella.

∽

"You the apprentices?" the broad-shouldered, bearded and belligerent carpenter asked of Pitty and his crew of three. The man stood in the doorway of a grand Georgian mansion, as big as any two such houses on average, occupying a choice address across from Holland Park in Kensington. The building had years ago been converted to a smart hotel named for the park, but even smart hotels begin to show wear after a time, and the Holland

Park Hotel had shut down for two weeks of filling cracks and painting walls and ceilings and the installation of modern plumbing and gas fixtures.

The carpenter, a man named Berk, was suspicious. There was nothing outwardly dubious about the four boys who had presented themselves for work that day, in fact, there was nothing even very distinctive about them. They all looked roughly like Pitty. They were dressed alike in flax trousers and shirts and cloth hats pulled low on their foreheads.

Berk was suspicious of the boys because Berk was suspicious of anyone who might claim some share of that which he expected to be paid for his work, and the work of the skilled and semi-skilled labourers that he hired for each job, depending on requirements. This particular job was already out of hand, and he was out-of-pocket by some considerable investment for people, pipes, and paint. In addition to being a comprehensive body of work, the hotel was a valuable building, and the owner had made it clear to Berk that any damage would either be repaired by Berk or paid for by Berk. That's why, painful as it was, Berk paid that smooth-talking Jacob Nightly tuppence a boy to have all the antique furniture moved out of each room as it was painted.

He wasn't going to have skilled labourers putting in time doing something a blind monkey could do, and he could charge the hotel owner for taking on four lads if he called them apprentices.

"Mister Nightly sent us, sir," said Pitty. "You asked for four smart lads, that's us."

"I asked for four strong lads," said Berk. "But if you can tell drapes from dunnage you'll do. It's like this, them lads over there, with paint all over 'em, they're going to paint every room of this hotel one by one. Before they does it, it's got to be cleared out of everything—every stick and wick, you understand?"

"Where do we put it?"

"In another room," said Berk with withering impatience. "One what's not being painted. I thought you said you was smart?"

"Sorry guvnor."

"Now, hop to it. And don't let me catch none of you idling, neither."

Berk didn't catch any of the Aldgate boys idling. In fact, whenever he poked his head into the hall one or more of them seemed to be going somewhere with some bit of furniture or bauble, and he had to admit that they seemed to be going about their work with immense care. So industrious were they, in fact, that it almost seemed as if there were eight boys moving valuable antique furniture about the hotel that day, all dressed exactly the same.

It was on the fourth day of plastering and painting that the hotel owner himself noticed the missing fixtures and furnishings. He picked his way through the ladders and tools and pots and brushes like the man he was—a wealthy man in an expensive suit dodging dangerously close to wet paint. He was tall, aquiline and circumspect, all features that were somehow compounded by his habit of wearing a monocle from which dangled a long, thin chain descending past his waist and swooping back up to hook into a buttonhole of his waistcoat.

"Berk, have you a moment?" said the owner from the doorway of the parlour, which Berk was busily converting into a modern grill room.

"Yes, sir, governor, sir, what may I do for you, sir?" Berk laid down his trowel and palette and swept his hat from his head.

"Those lads, moving my furniture about—why are there so many of them? And who's paying for them all?"

"They're the apprentices, sir, and they come cheap—tuppence each for the week."

"Cheapness is relative, Berk, what do they do for tuppence a week?"

"They do that as which a skilled labourer would be wasted in doing, if you please, sir," said Berk. "They move your delicate furnishings out of the way of the plaster and the paint, so as they shouldn't get damaged."

"For that I'm paying a shilling four a week, Berk?" said the hotelier. "That seems excessive, to me."

Berk nodded meditatively, as though weighing his employer's words, but he was in fact calculating tuppence times four and arriving at eightpence—less than a shilling four.

"Only eightpence, I think, sir."

"Eight boys times tuppence, you said, Berk," said the hotelier. "That's sixteen pence."

"Ah, there you are then, sir," said Berk, with enormous relief. "There's only the four lads."

"Eight, Berk. There are four there," the hotelier gestured across the hall to where Pitty and his crew were carefully covering a jumble of settees in drop cloths, "and I just saw another four go out through the kitchen carrying an armoire."

All enquiries were of course made, and before the hotelier, Berk and God, Pitty and his three fellow apprentices swore that there had only ever been four of them. They had seen four other boys, but they assumed that Berk had engaged them separately and, being as they were likely in competition, they elected to not socialise with the other boys who, in any case, appeared to be charged with moving all the more valuable items to safekeeping.

∼

THE OTHER FOUR boys didn't return the next day. Pitty did, and so did his crew, and so did the hotel owner, who was busily making an inventory of his losses. He was standing alone in the kitchen, making note of empty drawers and cabinets, when a figure appeared at the tradesman's entrance.

"Good day to you, sir," said what looked like a rag and bone man wearing his full stockpile of rags. "Are you the owner of this establishment?"

"I am. Who are you?"

"I'm called Sweeper, sir, and I've come to you with a business proposition."

"I see," said the hotelier, returning his attention to a ledger that he balanced in his left elbow. "The hotel is currently closed for renovations. If you have business with the kitchen staff, then you may return next week."

"Next week, you say, sir," said Sweeper. "That strikes me as a very ambitious schedule indeed."

"Ambitious?" The hotelier cast a suspicious eye over Sweeper.

"An hotel like this, reopening after a lengthy time, is going to need any number of items and materials, some of which you might not have accounted for in that there ledger, sir."

"Such as?"

"Silver service, for one, and silver porringers, pots, ice buckets... any number of copper kitchen utensils… three antique four-poster beds, complete with curtains… five armoires with mother-of-pearl-inlay… the list is quite exhaustive."

The hotelier closed his ledger and approached Sweeper. "Have you such a list?"

"I do, sir." Sweeper withdrew a cleanly folded sheet of paper from his pocket and handed it to the hotelier. "I think you'll find that it contains everything you could possibly need to get back in business right on time."

The hotelier took the list and examined it.

"What's to prevent me from turning you and this list over to the police?"

"The police?" Sweeper was aghast. "I've never been so insulted in my life. I'm an honest tradesman, in the business of recovering gently used hospitality equipment and supplies and returning them to service. I come into these effects in good faith, sir, though I have no means with which to speak to the faith of those what sold them to me."

"Very well then," said the hotelier, leaning menacingly toward Sweeper. "What's to prevent me from giving you the thrashing you so richly deserve?"

"Business, sir," said Sweeper. "I count on your cool judgement to stop you doing something rash that would serve neither of our interests, Mister… might I know your name, sir, if it's going to come to blows?"

"Blythe," said the hotelier, as though the name carried weight. "Max Blythe."

"Max Blythe?" said Sweeper, as though the name carried considerable weight. "I think I knew your cousin, sir, in India."

The man now known as Max Blythe stepped back out of the zone of menace.

"You knew Matthew Blythe?"

"I did sir," said Sweeper. "A great tragedy, what happened to him."

"How could a man like you come to know my cousin?"

"I worked in Jaipur in the day, sir. I was handyman to Mister Blythe and a number of similarly occupied gentlemen and their families. Handyman Sweet, they called me, for I can tell you now, sir, that is my real name."

"Your real name is Handyman?"

"My real name is Cyril Sweet, but I was called Handyman Sweet during my days in Jaipur."

"I see," said Blythe. "And you say that you were there when he died?"

"Not by his side, no," said Sweeper. "But I was on hand when the girl was kidnapped. It was very much, and very clearly, the beginning of the end. It was me what carried notes to you to the maritime telegraph office, and hence how I recognise your name now."

"I see."

"You've done all right for yourself." Sweeper stepped into the kitchen and looked around at the gleaming new tiles.

"And just what do you mean by that?"

Sweeper smiled meaningfully at Blythe. "I carried the telegrams in both directions, Mister Blythe. I remember that you was always asking your cousin for money. Didn't you have some trouble with a lawsuit for breach of contract?"

"How dare you!"

"I beg your pardon, sir," said Sweeper, still smiling. "It's only that I find it ironic that you come out of India so much better off than your cousin, in spite of never having gone in."

"It was his decision to transplant an English wife and child into that alien land. Some such tragedy was bound to happen."

"Not such a tragedy for you though, was it, Mister Blythe?" Sweeper was wandering through the kitchen, now, and marvelling at its size.

"You'd be wise to weigh your words more carefully, Handyman Sweet."

"Sweeper, if you please, sir. I left the name Handyman Sweet in India and came home to be a street sweeper."

"I thought you were a duffer."

"I can be honest with you, Mister Blythe, I am a duffer. I only handle the finest quality of stolen merchandise, but I am a duffer, nonetheless. However, the occupation of street sweeper is an honourable one, and I can hardly call myself Duffer Sweet, can I?"

"Nevertheless, your trade is selling back that which was stolen," said Blythe. "That's a very clever system that you've developed—in acquiring the supply you create the demand."

"T'is clever, but I can't take the credit," admitted Sweeper. "I only go where I'm sent and offer what I'm given."

"I hope you don't mean to tell me that you're in no position to return that which is rightfully mine."

"Oh, I can do much better than that, I believe."

"What do you mean, Duffer?"

"This hotel, Mister Blythe, it's all yours, is it?"

"Among others, yes."

"Very impressive. And after all that trouble you had while your cousin was in India. Lucky for you he died when he did. You must have come into a considerable fortune."

"And what of it? He died without issue. It's sad, but there it is."

"There you have it, Mister Blythe—he didn't."

"Of course, he did. I received the death certificate from the Jaipur authorities, signed by Doctor Halliwell himself."

"Of course, Matthew Blythe died. I saw the body myself." Sweeper caught Blythe's eye. "Very nasty."

"He was drowned, I understand."

"He was, but it is not this to which I refer when I say, 'he didn't'. I was correcting your misapprehension that your cousin died without issue."

"You mean Bethany? Surely it's taken as fact that she was murdered by her kidnappers."

"That is, indeed, the generally received understanding of affairs, sir," confirmed Sweeper. "I'm in a position to inform you, though, that his daughter—and rightful heir—is still alive to this day."

CHAPTER 10

A BOLT OF SILK

By April of 1879 the Clerkenwell Working Orphanage was eight years behind Stella and would have been largely given over to the mists of time, but for the anchor. In idle moments or when a bell rang or she caught a glance of the river or a prison, Stella thought of Teddy, and that made her think of the orphanage with a fondness that defied reason. She never wanted to see the orphanage again and, above all, she never again wanted to remember herself as that vulnerable and governed, but the orphanage was where she went when she thought of Teddy. It was where he lived, still, in her memories, and it was the only place where she could go and talk to him or just lie next to him on a recollection of a bale of hay.

Stella couldn't resign herself to never seeing Teddy again, but she nevertheless convinced herself that was the case. She'd never see anyone from the orphanage again—that was the sacrifice, the price she paid to be her own person. If she didn't seek it out then it would stay in the past, and she'd be safe from it. Thusly determined, Stella was unprepared when her life as an orphan came looking for her.

⁓

"You the apprentices from Mister Nightly?"

Stella, Lucy, and Emma curtsied clumsily before Gretta Steep, a tall, severe woman with a face like an outraged brougham horse, and she glared down at the girls as though it was they who had brought offence. "You look like street urchins. I don't find it credible that you're experienced seamstresses."

"Yes, Miss Steep," said Stella. "We wasn't told you wanted girls who could dress just so, just girls who could sew dresses."

"Are you being flippant with me, you mop-haired waif?"

"No, madam, not deliberately."

"Because if you are, you can go right back to Mister Nightly and tell him to return my nine pence."

"Beg pardon, Miss Steep."

The woman stared hard into Stella's eyes, as though searching for remaining traces of audacity. It was an act, of course, and this woman was no more able to send away three girls who may have been qualified seamstresses any more than she was able to return to her employer and tell him that he was a mazy scrub. The effect, in either case, would be the same, even though her employer was widely known as a mazy scrub, and even though Miss Steep was already managing no fewer than thirteen regular girls. Time was short, and the challenge of getting these girls into the workshop remained formidable.

Miss Steep stood in the shadow of the alley separating two grand shops on the Strand. The alley only extended as far as the back of the buildings, where it met the grate of a man-sized storm drain which drained the Strand of rainwater, directing any risk of flooding into the Thames. The alley, consequently, was a cul-de-sac, and it was dark and discreet, but the sun was rising and quickly burning off the fog and splashing rays of Spring morning sun dangerously near.

"I'm going to walk down this alley. You will follow me but not so close as to give the impression that we know each other."

"Yes, madam," said all three girls in harmony.

"When I enter the workshop, I will leave the door open. Wait a moment, then follow. Once you're inside you must remain perfectly quiet and you must not leave that room, for any reason, do you understand?"

"I guess we understand the instruction, madam, without understanding the reasoning," answered Stella.

"The reasoning is none of your business," said Miss Steep, but continued, nevertheless. "You will be working for a very prestigious society clothier, attaching fancies to dresses for a quality wedding. The ceremony is on Saturday, and it's imperative that the work is done—correctly, mind—by the end of tomorrow, to allow time for alterations."

"Yes, Miss Steep."

"There are four sewing machines and everything you need, but for the dresses. I will bring you the dresses when they're ready and when it's safe to do so. You must, by no account, be seen on the shop floor. The bride herself, Isobel Merriman, will often visit, to personally oversee the details, do you know who that is?"

"No, Miss Streep," said the girls in harmony, but for Stella, the name rang a distant bell.

"This is just as well, it's enough that you know that she must not know that we have engaged provisional assistance, particularly girls of your... of your qualifications. Is that clear?"

"Yes, Miss Steep."

"For your own sake, and for that of Mister Nightly and his future hopes of doing business with this enterprise, I hope that it is," scolded Miss Steep. "Now, wait until I'm near that door, right there, and then follow."

Miss Steep turned on her heel and stalked purposely up the alley toward The Strand. The girls shared a mischievous smile.

"What's the lay, Stella?" asked Lucy.

"Don't know yet. Never been here before, have you?"

"No," answered both Emma and Lucy.

"Got to be plenty worth taking, though," added Lucy.

"Then that's the lay," said Stella. "Work for real, keep your eyes open, worst we come out of it is tuppence each."

Happily, there was, indeed, plenty worth taking. Beyond the door in the alley of the building giving onto the Strand, was a storage room that had been adapted to serve as a concealed workshop. There was a door to the outside and a door to what sounded like a busy, mechanised workshop, and the only natural light came from a window above the exterior door. There were also three good sewing machines, scissors, thread, and spools of ribbon to be formed into golden bows and silk bridesmaid's dresses, and there were high shelves creaking with reams of fine silk, crepe, and bombazine.

The girls checked their machines and made a mental evaluation of the inventory and were sitting attentively when Miss Steep returned. She opened the clapboard door a crack, pushed herself through, and pulled the door closed behind her.

"Can you sew ribbon?" she asked.

"Yes, Miss Steep," answered Stella. "From this?" She referred to a ream leaning against her machine, wrapped in what had to be an excess of golden silk.

"Yes, that's right," said Miss Steep, allowing a subtle sag of relief into her face and voice. "Twelve of them. Two yards, eight inches long, eight inches wide."

"Eight inches, Miss?" said Stella.

Miss Steep snapped a paper into view and stared at it as though it contained a shocking headline.

"Quite right," she said. "Four inches. Eight inches folded."

"Eight and an eighth, I think," suggested Stella. "To allow for the seam."

"Yes, very well, eight and an eighth."

"Twelve silk ribbons, two yards eight inches long and four inches wide, with a single inside seam."

"Yes. Excellent," said Miss Steep. "It's imperative… it's very important that they be done by ten o'clock. It's seven o'clock now. Can you manage?"

"Oh, yes, madame," said Stella. "Perhaps you could check on us at nine o'clock, to be certain that we've followed your instructions correctly."

"Yes. Yes, that's what I'll do. Just what I was going to do."

Miss Steep looked around at the girls, bit her knuckle, then slipped back out the door.

"Emma," whispered Stella. "We'll do the ribbons you get to the market hall at Covent Garden. Pitty's there today, selling dollymops."

"How does Pitty know dollymops?"

"He don't, does he?" said Stella. "He just finds blokes what look lonely, points out some nice bit of bird, and tells him she's got reduced rates on Tuesdays, but he's got to pay up front."

"What do I want with Pitty, then?"

"Tell him to pinch a dory and have it under Waterloo Bridge tonight by dark. He's got a boatload of silk to take to the *Maltsack*."

RIBBONS WERE sewn and approved by Miss Steep. Then more ribbons were made and then they were all formed into bows and carefully hung in anticipation of fixing them to twelve matching dresses the following day. Through the door, Stella could hear work winding down as, she estimated, some dozen seamstresses finished for the day. The light from the exterior window went in an instant from afternoon grey to stormy black, and Stella turned up the kerosene lamps. Taps of rain clicked on the glass, then intensified into a drumbeat, and within minutes had become an unbroken torrent.

"Off you go," said Stella to Lucy and Emma. "Lucy, go to the bridge and bring Pitty back here, then wait until I give the signal, then come and carry what you can."

"That won't be very much," observed Lucy.

"Don't need to be. We're only taking the gold silk."

"What's that worth?" asked Emma.

"Probably ha'penny a yard, usually," said Stella. "But if this workshop has to deliver a dozen gold silk dresses for a society wedding by day after tomorrow, you can bet they'll pay ten times that, and think it a bargain. Now, go."

The door clicked and rattled, and Stella plucked a pair of detail scissors from the working table. She was examining the bows as Miss Steep slipped into the room.

THE GRAVEST OF MISFORTUNES

"That's enough," she said. "You may go, now, and be back here at seven in the morning."

"I'll just finish detailing these bows, Miss Steep," said Stella. "That way we can get an early start."

Miss Steep squinted in the fading light.

"Very well, but be quick about it," she said. "I'll be back shortly to lock that door." She slipped back out the door and pulled it shut.

Stella quickly and quietly pulled a heavy ream of thick linen from a shelf, laid it on the floor and unwound and cut six, three-yard lengths, and she used those to wrap the delicate silk against the rain. The rain would render the silk unusable, otherwise, and not even worth stealing. She wrapped the first two bolts of golden silk and tied them off with twine, and then went to the outside door, pushed it open, put her fingers to her mouth, and issued a quick, sharp whistle. Pitty and Lucy emerged from the shadows and Stella handed them each a ream.

"Take that to the boat, then come right back."

She closed the door and listened. Voices and shuffling indicated that Miss Steep and someone else remained in the workshop. Stella bent quickly to her work, and began wrapping another ream, and she was wrapping the second when the workshop door opened. Through the door Stella could see only darkness—the workshop was unlit, now—but she knew that the figure in the doorway wasn't Miss Steep.

"Stella?"

Stella stood and squinted in the darkness. The light from the lamp lit her face but turned the other into a silhouette, and yet a series of epiphanies came to her and in an instant she knew that she was looking at the workshop of Montague and Cruikshank, Ladies' Clothiers, and the girl in the doorway was Mathilda Corbit.

"Matty," exclaimed Stella in a hushed cry. She dropped the linen sheet and rushed to the door and threw her arms around her old friend.

"Stella… what are you doing here?" asked Matty. In her confusion, she couldn't bring herself to return Stella's affection.

"Working," said Stella, stepping back from the embrace. "Making these ribbons."

"I know. I'm the head seamstress. We're making the bridesmaid's dresses. I didn't know that it was you—Miss Steep only said that there were three urchins doing the detailing. Where are the others?"

At that, the outside door burst in with a clatter and boom of rain and thunder, and Pitty and Lucy stumbled through.

"Them's the next to go, Stella?" asked Pitty.

"No, Pitty, wait outside," said Stella quickly but without conviction.

"Stella, what are you doing?" asked Matty.

"Listen, Matty, we're taking the silk, but you have nothing to worry about—tomorrow a duffer's going to sell them back to the shop."

"No, Stella, you can't." Matty's voice was a shout, now, and Stella knew that there was no turning back.

"Matty, please…"

"Miss Steep!" Matty stepped back, away from her old friend. "Miss Steep, get Mister Abernathy, quick, there's a robbery!"

"Oh, Matty…" Stella turned to Lucy and Pitty. "Take those two, run!"

Pitty and Stella snatched up the two bolts and fumbled out into the rain. Already in the alley there was shouting, and Stella pictured the mousetrap into which she'd just sent Lucy and Pitty—the alley was a cul-de-sac, giving out onto the Strand. At the other end was a storm drain, blocked by an iron grate. This Mister Abernathy would be able to block any escape to the street.

Now Miss Steep was in the doorway behind Matty, and so Stella dashed out into the alley. The tempest was everything and everywhere. It was like diving into the sea. The rain crashed onto the paving stones and the thunder roared overhead and echoed into the alley. The gaslights in the street made sharp silhouettes of a tall, spidery man facing Lucy and Pitty who, cast long, mad shadows that danced and dodged as Mister Abernathy moved to block their escape.

True to their training, Lucy and Pitty threw the reams of fabric into the air. The wind ripped away the linen protection and the golden silk fell to the alley with a wet slap.

THE GRAVEST OF MISFORTUNES

"No!" shouted Matty from the door. "Stella, what have you done!"

Stella and Matty shared a look of betrayal. At the end of the alley Pitty and Lucy outmanoeuvred Mister Abernathy and disappeared into a wall of rain. Mister Abernathy instead set his sights on Stella. She ran to a door on the opposing wall and, of course, it was locked. Mister Abernathy approached slowly and carefully—he wasn't going to let the ringleader escape a prison sentence for the damage these thieves had done. Stella backed away in vain—she knew that there was no escape. Finally, she ran out of alley, and her back was against the iron bars of the storm drain. A rush of overflow from the Strand surged down the middle of the alley and poured over Stella's feet and into the drain. Mister Abernathy bore down on her like a bear in the rain. A burst of lightning lit his face and Stella fancied that she saw, briefly, madness for revenge.

"Please..." Stella started to say, but in that moment the bars of the storm drain fell away and Stella fell with them. In an instant, she was in darkness, and someone was holding her tightly and dragging her heels through the silt and debris of the tunnel. Over the rush of the current Stella could hear Mister Abernathy's frustrated shouts echoing away.

Stella regained her feet, and she was running next to her saviour, who held her hand and guided her down slippery brick steps, on either side of which water drained toward the river. Finally, they were in the mouth of the storm drain, next to the gardens named for the Victoria Embankment. The overflow rushed over their feet, but they were soaked to the skin, and it made little difference that they were in some degree of shelter from the rain, which formed a curtain so thick that they could barely see the river, boiling beneath the tempest.

Stella's heart beat hard and fast, and she held onto her saviour. He held her back, tightly, and before she looked up into his eyes, she knew that she was holding onto none other than Teddy Tooter.

CHAPTER 11

CANUTE AND THE TIDE

"Where are we?"

Stella and Teddy were sat on a riverbank, as near as Stella could tell, but they were also underground. The storm had subsided, but the little river still rushed and splashed with runoff, and the bank was formed of rough paving stones. The rippling of the river echoed off the stone walls and ceiling, and the sound and atmosphere were unlike anything Stella had ever known.

Teddy had built a fire within a circle of rocks between them and the shivering and clattering of teeth were finally sufficiently reduced for Stella to pose the questions which played upon her mind.

"River Fleet," said Teddy, carefully layering his fire with bits of driftwood, raising immediately the level of heat and flame. "Underneath Blackfriars Road."

Teddy stood, turned to the darkness, and then returned with a blanket, which he draped around Stella's shoulders. She could finally focus on his face, which was uncannily the same as it was when she'd last seen it seven years before, and yet it was nevertheless that of a young man. He was clean-shaven and broad of face and shoulder, just as he'd promised to be as a boy, and his rain-matted hair was short and raggedy.

"How do you know about this place?" asked Stella. "No, forget about that. Where have you been? How have you been?"

"Same answer to all three questions. I've been underground. They sent me to the Soap Pits, but I was already too big to be a hurrier and too small to be a getter, and then they started on the new sewerage system for London, so they sent me back here."

"Why haven't I seen you until now?"

Teddy smiled a sad, cynical smile. "Not for lack of trying, Stella. I went back to the orphanage, peeked through the gate on Sundays, but you was never there."

"I ran away."

Teddy nodded, as though that's exactly what he'd assumed for seven years.

"Turns out London's bigger than we thought."

"I don't suppose it is," said Stella. "You was right where I needed you to be tonight."

"That weren't luck. I remembered Montague and Cruikshank. I thought you would, too, so I waited outside some nights and talked to Matty. She didn't know where you were, neither."

"I didn't look for her," said Stella. "I didn't think I'd do her much good."

Again, Teddy nodded sagely. "I reckoned you would one day, though. I have no place else to be, most nights."

"You've been living underground for seven years?"

"No," Teddy laughed. "I'm a navvy, aren't I. It's a regular job. Three shillings a week, less a shilling for room and board."

"You were going to be royalty."

Teddy shrugged the corners of his mouth.

"I got that laughed out of me in the sewers. You were the last person to ever believe in me."

"Good thing you found me, then," said Stella. "I knew you would, you know."

Teddy looked up from the fire and it reflected itself in his eye.

"I know," he said. "I knew it too. Didn't think it would take this long, but I don't suppose I knew how long it was going to take." He balanced another bit of driftwood on the fire. "I missed you, Stella. I didn't miss nothing or no one else, but I missed you like my own eyes."

"Me too, Teddy.

"Looked all over—you can get just about anywhere underground, you know, London's built over a dozen rivers like the Fleet. Where was you?"

"I was all over, too. Are the sisters still at Clerkenwell?"

Teddy nodded. "I was there only last Sunday. Saw Matron and Sister Margaret."

"How did they look?"

"Only saw them for a brief moment." Teddy smiled mischievously. "I threw a rock at the prison bell."

Stella threw her head back and laughed. "Nothing could please me more. Does it still work?"

Teddy's smile fell and away and his eyes dropped to the fire.

"I missed."

∽

By that Spring the offices of the Aldgate Apprenticeship were back in the yard of Saint Botolph's, with high-level committee meetings in the mausoleum of the Reed family, long time patrons of the church. When Stella and Teddy arrived murmurs of dissent had already begun.

"You're late," pointed out Jacob Nightly. "Who's this?"

"Teddy Tooter," said Stella. "He's an irregular."

"He looks it," said Pitty. He stood to Jacob's right, and would do while Twick served a year in the workhouse for spending forged notes.

"Is this the lad who ruined last night's carefully conceived plan at Montague and Cruikshank?" asked Jacob.

"It was my plan, and I made it up on the spot," said Stella. "And why didn't you tell me that it was Montague and Cruikshank?"

"Would it have made a difference?"

Stella looked from Jacob to Teddy and back again. "Yes, Jacob, more than you know."

"What happened?"

"We ruined a society wedding, and Teddy saved me from getting pinched. Did you know that there's a whole underground river system underneath the city, and that you can go anywhere you like without no one seeing you?"

"There's never," protested Pitty.

"No, wait, I've heard something of this," said Jacob, stroking his beard, which was still greasy but now grey, too. "Does this Teddy Tooter know his way around this network?"

"Like no other," said Stella. "He's a navvy. A canal navvy, building the London sewerage system."

"That would explain the smell. Could your friend wait outside, Stella?" said Pitty.

"Quiet, Pitty, I'm sure that Stella still has eyes only for your Byronic beauty," said Jacob. "He's a big lad, too. I suppose they have you doing a lot of digging."

"Not so much as you might think, sir," said Teddy, and the assembly broke into peals of laughter at this honorific bestowed on Jacob. Teddy waited, baffled, until order restored itself. "It's mostly shifting rocks, you see."

"We could use an irregular this Sunday who's good at shifting heavy things. A shilling for a day's work—are you interested?"

"Yes, sir, thank you, sir," said Teddy, but the novelty of hearing Jacob called 'sir' had worn thin.

"Here's the lay, then," said Jacob. "There's a bottler in Bermondsey filling an order for a society party—might even be this wedding, if it's still on. They've got nobody to work Sundays, so we're providing them two strong lads and two smart girls. All you've got to do is fill bottles from a keg, put them in crates, then the boys stack the crates, wait for a gig, load it up with the crates, the day's over."

"What's the lay, then?" asked Pitty. "Do we nick the gig?"

"No, of course…" Jacob stopped himself and stroked his beard while he considered this, "…No, we don't nick the gig. That's horse-thievery and they hang you for that. No, we'll nick as many crates as we can during the day. Stands to reason there won't be much in the way of supervision, being a Sunday, so whenever you get a chance, you just put a crate outside. While you're waiting for the gig, you run them down to the river. I'll be there with a dory."

"Not much of a plan, though, is it Jacob?" said Stella.

"Oh? I suppose you'd have us nearly get nicked, and smash as many bottles as we can before running away, would you?"

"Someone's bound to see the boys stacking crates of wine *outside* the place," Stella pointed out. "Every crate's a risk of getting caught for twelve bottles of wine."

"You say Bermondsey," interjected Teddy. "Where in Bermondsey?"

"Shad Thames," said Jacob.

"Riverside or wharf side?"

"Wharf."

"I might have a better idea, Jacob," said Teddy.

"I'm not too proud. What is it?"

"The bottlers is right next to Canute's Trench," explained Teddy. "The River Neckinger. It's buried, now, but at Shad Thames it's an inlet. When the tide's out, it's just mud."

"How does that help us?"

"Noon Sunday is lowest tide. Whenever we get a chance, we roll a whole keg out the door and into the trench. It'll sink into the mud and be hidden almost right away. The only risk is when we're rolling it out the door. Then the tide rises. By five o'clock the barrel will be floating."

"And we row in and pick it up," concluded Jacob.

"Just so," said Teddy. "And if there's time and quantity, we can push out as many kegs as the trench can swallow."

CHAPTER 12

THE DEMISE OF THE DE VEERS DESCENDANCY

*B*ermondsey Bottling, to the trade, was the product of a turbulent history, at least by the standards of a bottling plant. Started as a bespoke glassblower in the early part of the century by transplanted Dutchman Anton de Veers, it was soon doing a brisk trade in bottles and flagons to the hospitality industry of south London. By the time Anton passed the business along to his two sons, the family name had become De Veers and the size and shape of bottles had become uniform. The business grew and divided further, among Anton's grandchildren, and the bottling was finally brought in-house, and it was performed in a newly acquired factory space on Shad Thames in Bermondsey, and simultaneously renamed Bermondsey Bottling, as a compromise between factions which were now composed of no less than four different family names. Varying degrees of interest in the bottling industry were not reflected in the equal shares held by the diverse descendants of Anton de Veers, many of whom were satisfied with drawing down dividends from the business, leading to considerable conflict with the faction of the family which wanted to reinvest and expand.

In lieu of compromise, those who preferred their gratification immediate turned to the credit markets, specifically a City financier called Del Daly, who provided them with ready capital, collateralised by their interest in Bermondsey Bottling. When these loans were gambled and drunk and frittered into default, Mister Daly became the principal shareholder in Bermondsey Bottling, and he drove out the remaining bickering traces of a once-proud name in glassblowing.

Among the first orders of business for the new, hands-on operator of Bermondsey Bottling to the trade was to renew relationships with the trade, which had been soured by inconsistent and often belligerent management. Del Daly used his City contacts to offer a generous price of nothing at all to

THE GRAVEST OF MISFORTUNES

the newly constructed Langley Hotel in Grosvenor Square, which in turn was sharply discounting its services as a caterer to the society wedding of the year. The tumble-down effect was that the Sunday prior to the wedding, Del Daly needed help getting wine out of kegs and into bottles.

∼

"Only four of you?"

Del Daly didn't appear to be anyone's idea of a bottler nor, for that matter, a City financier. He was short and compact, like a barrel full of something solid. His head was bald but for enormous sideburns that wrapped themselves all the way around from one side to the other and very nearly met again just above his upper lip. He dressed like a member of the idle class, but he had the accent and demeanour of a dockworker, and he somehow managed to keep the sleeves of his coat pushed up on his forearms.

"Two smart girls and two strong boys, sir," said Stella. "Is that not what you asked for?"

"I suppose I did," said Daly. "For some reason I expected four to amount to more than you lot. Still, you look like strong lads and apt girls, and we've got this morning and afternoon to empty six kegs into sixteen hundred bottles." As he spoke Daly turned and led the way through the carriage-sized doors of his share of a factory building, accessible from Shad Thames and, from the opposing side, Canute's Trench.

The inside was a vast chaos of shelves and kegs and crates of bottles and corks. There were barrows for shifting full kegs, pipes and picks and valves for draining them into bottles, and there were shelves stacked high as a house with barrels. Pitty tried to catch Stella's eye to share a hungry glance, but she was paying studious attention to Daly's instructions.

"Each barrel's a good hogshead—that means no less than two hundred and sixty bottles, twenty-two crates. Six barrels should be a hundred and thirty crates. You lads shift a barrel—starting from the top of the back shelf—and stack the crates there, at the door. This evening a gig comes to take them away."

"One gig for a hundred and thirty crates of wine?" asked Stella, scepticism in what she said but not how she said it.

"One gig for fifty crates of wine," corrected Daly. "I have many friends, and it's the wise man what seizes an opportunity to ply his friends and fellows with wine."

Work was slow to start, largely because nobody, including Daly, knew how to get a keg weighing over four hundred pounds from a high shelf, and considerable time was lost speculating how it got up there. Eventually, a rope and pulley were spotted hanging from rails attached to the ceiling, and work was begun.

"I've looked," said Teddy to Stella when they were alone together figuring out the pipe and valve system. "There's a door behind them shelves on the other side of the hall."

"That Daly bloke likes to be on hand, don't he?" Stella cast a meaningful glance over her shoulder at Del Daly, who had positioned himself strategically at the entrance to the factory floor with a prison-guard view of the kegging and decanting activities. He had occupied this position for the entire morning and most of the afternoon, and Stella was decanting the fourth barrel. Some seventy crates of wine were stacked neatly by the door, and the gig could be along at any time.

"What we want is a bell." Teddy smiled at the shared recollection.

"You're right, that's exactly what we need." Stella handed Teddy a length of pipe to give the impression that work was being done. "Can you take down another keg, before this one's done, and then another after that?"

"'Course I can."

"Then get them ready to roll over here. Tell Pitty—when I give the signal, he rolls the keg toward me, but it gets away from him, and it goes right out that door."

Teddy glanced furtively toward the wide stable doors at the front of the factory and traced the path back to the barrels.

"And when Daly and Pitty are chasing after it, I roll the extra keg out the back."

"And into the mud," said Stella. "Can you do it?"

"'Course I can." Teddy's voice had something of the bravado of the boy who would be king, and Stella instinctively put her hand over his and looked into his eyes. Teddy returned the fond regard, and his chest and shoulders swelled to the task ahead.

. . .

"Look out!" shouted Pitty, as four hundred pounds of wood and wine bounced and bounded across the uneven floor of the factory.

"Stop it, you corn-faced gallumpus." Daly kept pace next to the barrel as it rolled toward the door, but he knew better than to stand in its way. The clatter and excitement of two men chasing a rampant keg made for a distraction to the sound of the rear door opening and Teddy carefully rolling out a barrel.

The escaped keg continued at large, right out the door and into the street, with Pitty now in close pursuit and Daly behind him, hurling condemnations of the boy's intelligence, aptitude, and parentage. The drama ended, as so many do, without incident. The street on that Sunday afternoon was empty, and it was formed of a soft depression allowing for a gutter. The barrel passed over the little valley, rolled up the other side, was called to a stop by gravity, and then rolled back, and then repeated this like a pendulum until it was finally becalmed.

Pitty and Daly rolled the keg back into the factory. Stella and Lucy returned to their work. The plan appeared to have unfolded exactly as expected, but when Stella glanced toward the back of the factory, she saw no sign of Teddy. Her response was the practised nonchalance of a career con artist. She returned to her work. Lucy handed her another bottle. Pitty rolled the barrel back into place. Work went on. The day wore on into evening, and still Teddy hadn't returned, and more worrisome still, Daly made no remark on the issue.

Finally, the last drop of wine fell into the last bottle, it was placed in a crate, and that crate was stacked with the others.

"Right, you two, get lucky," said Stella to Lucy and Pitty. "Just walk out like nothing's happened. Like you never knew no one called Teddy."

As Lucy and Pitty walked calmly out the front door and into the street, they were passed, coming in the other direction, by a long, low gig, pulled by a stout Clydesdale, and ridden by no fewer than four terrifying figures.

The events and peculiarities of the past few days came to Stella in a single sinister premonition. She was finally reunited with Teddy but betrayed by Matty. She lost and destroyed the silk for the bridesmaids' dresses. Her life had been weaving itself into this society wedding in some way known only to the fates, who were preparing some complex machine of darkest irony. Isobel Merryman was getting married next week, to some peer of the realm, but that was not the distant bell that rang for Stella when she heard the name. Only now, when she saw the royal blue uniforms and silk top hats of the men dismounting from the gig did she recall that Isobel Merryman's father was Alexander Lord Merryman, head of the London Metropolitan Police.

"Where's that other lad going?" Daly called to Stella. An honest question, but there was something knowing and nefarious in his voice. "He's not done 'til the gig is loaded up."

"Teddy can do it, sir," said Stella, her voice chiming with innocence.

Daly approached Stella. "He's in no position to do that, now, is he?"

"I don't know what you mean, sir." Stella looked around her, as though only then noticing that she was a man short.

Daly crossed his arms over his chest and leaned back against an imaginary wall of moral authority.

"You're the smart one, aren't you, girl?"

"I certainly hope you're satisfied with our work today, Mister Daly."

"Very, thanks." Daly looked over his shoulder at the policemen as they loaded crates of wine onto the gig. "But you can tell Mister Nightly that I won't be paying the remainder."

"Very good, sir," said Stella.

"Now, let's go see how that bludger of yours is doing…" Daly swept past Stella toward the back of the factory. She glanced at the door and the busy constables, weighed her options, and then followed.

The tide had risen in Canute's trench and, as Teddy had predicted, the barrel of wine had risen with it. Teddy was in the water up to his waist, tying off the keg with rope, and on the dock above him were two uniformed constables with top-hats, stern looks, and bludgeons.

Teddy glanced up, then, with fear and foreboding. He had been back in Stella's life little more than a day, and in that time, she'd managed to destroy all his prospects.

"I'll ask you again," said Daly to Stella. "Who's the smart one?"

"I don't know what you mean, sir."

"Whose idea was it to cop a hogshead from Del Daly?" said Daly. "You see, I think you're the brains behind this outfit, and I look forward to watching your future career with interest. Whose idea was it? I ask chiefly out of curiosity, you understand." Daly jerked his head in the general direction of the trench. "Either way, it's the end of the line for that lad."

CHAPTER 13

THE RELEASE OF RIPLEY STANDISH

It took until October of 1863 for Ripley Standish to reach his limits. He'd exhausted his strength and intellect and the goodwill of many of his friends and financiers as he endeavoured to run the various enterprises, he had established with his late friend Matthew Blythe. It was chiefly Matthew's technical expertise that was missed, but Rip knew that he had lost his flair and passion for the work, and so the managerial and diplomatic side of things was slipping too. His old instincts for flattery and brinkmanship were leaving him, and it was only a matter of time before he made some grave mistake.

Shipments of marble were arriving short from the Delhi Territory. Workmanship had declined precipitously on projects across the city. No new contracts were forthcoming. The only way to save the business, Rip realised with calm relief, was to abandon it.

Rip had been able to liquidate Matthew Blythe's holdings because there was something to hold, but now the only remaining avenue was a careful winding down. Rip sold his leases and contracts, and he converted his assets to certificate shares in other concerns. His last act in Jaipur was to invite Brother Uckeridge to live in his house, for as long as the missionary had need of accommodation and at least until Rip returned from a farewell tour of the territories. In exchange, Brother Uckeridge would watch over the boy.

The rebellion was five years in the past and a Jodhpur railway was forty years in the future, and so travel between Jaipur and Makrana was a matter of a well-armed convoy of horses and two days' circuitous travel to make a journey that would otherwise have taken a day, even on foot. At the time, Makrana marble was expensive and oversubscribed, and so Rip had long ago made arrangements to found a new quarry to the west, in the territory nominally claimed by Jat tribesmen.

This was the early, skittish days of Jat homesteading in northern India, and a delicate matrix of British, princely, and tribal rule overlapped across the territory. The Jat were of a martial heritage and not timid about resorting to war, and hence they remained largely autonomous. Years ago, Rip had exploited this ambiguous legal state to form supply lines of marble sliced out of the ground around Makrana, matching its quality at a fraction of its price.

Rip's escort went no further than the tiny, industrious city of Makrana, and he continued with four horses and three trusted members of his staff, including Alem, who appeared to speak all languages known to man.

The evening sun was throwing long shadows behind them as the party arrived at the scattered buildings and pits that comprised the ad hoc village of Sangam. By reflex, the horses increased their canter as they sensed rest and water, and the cracking and scraping of the refinishing of marble grew louder.

"You will present this walking stick, Mister Ripley," announced Alem, withdrawing from his saddlebag a glistening cane. "It is understood that Rajmata

Rajmata has acquired a limp since we last saw her, owing to an accident in the quarry."

Rajmata Rajmata was the dowager of Sangam, mother to the late Rajmata and in turn grandmother to the boy who would one day call himself Marahajah. In the meantime, she was the effective chief of a small tribe of quarriers, and an invaluable asset to the continuing affairs of Blythe and Standish.

"Isn't that in rather poor taste, Mister Alem?"

"It is understood that Rajmata Rajmata is quite proud of the injury," replied Alem. "She is over sixty years old and continues to be among the more productive workers in the quarry. At any rate, you will notice that the walking stick is purely ornamental. It was conceived and crafted to appeal to the martial traditions of the Jat."

Alem reached for the stick between the horses. Rip took it and observed that it was, indeed, an impractical cane, but an extraordinarily ornate example of detailed goldsmithing. The stick was heavy oak but smoothly balanced by a golden handle, wound in a tapered, relief depiction of the history of the quarry at Sangam.

The sun was fully set as they rode into the village. Work ceased, and cooking fires were lit, and laughter and chatter filled the air. Alem sought and received directions to Rajmata Rajmata, and the party continued across what amounted to a dusty village square to a newly thatched house.

"Rajmata Rajmata, I feel that it's been years, and yet if anything you look younger than ever." Rip knew that Alem would translate this as something appreciably more appropriate, but he also knew that his sincere expression of bonhomie would travel a lot further and do a great deal more good than empty flattery.

Rajmata Rajmata did not look younger than the last time Rip had seen her, but she didn't look any older, either. Since he'd first laid eyes on her, some ten years previously, she'd appeared to be about a hundred years old, just as she did now. But she had a winning, if uneven, smile, and she somehow wore her wrinkles like royal gowns. She was otherwise simply dressed in heavy, faded weaves and her hair, white with years and quarry dust, was in a single, thick braid. She was sitting on a simple wooden chair as though it was a throne, and she was attended by a young girl of perhaps ten years old.

THE GRAVEST OF MISFORTUNES

Rip and Alem stood before her, having left their own attendants to care for the horses.

"I heard about your injury, acquired on our behalf," continued Rip, holding up the walking stick in two hands, "and so I rushed to your side with this, so that it might not slow you down."

Even as Alem translated this the old queen leapt to her feet and took the cane from Rip.

She spoke warmly and breathlessly. Alem translated this as "Rajmata Rajmata welcomes her honoured guest and accepts this gift worthy of a queen."

She examined the cane with one hand on the oak and another gripping the golden handle, and then by some instinct she knew to twist it. The mechanism clicked and separated, and Rajmata Rajmata shared a mischievous smile with Rip. She drew the handle away, and it was followed by a long and gleaming blade. She bowed ceremoniously toward Rip, restored the blade to its sheath, and returned to her chair. She bade her visitors sit, and then gave instructions to the girl. The girl ran off into the night, and within moments tribal elders were joining the party in the increasingly enclosed space. Alem was put through his paces interpreting and relaying greetings and platitudes.

"My dear Rajmata Rajmata," said Rip, holding a cup of tea as though about to propose a toast. "I confess that I didn't just come to bring you that walking stick."

Alem translated and the queen-mother smiled warmly.

"In fact, I came to bring you a gift of much, much greater value," continued Rip. He waited while Alem translated this, and the assemblage leaned forward in uniform curiosity. Rip withdrew a long, stiff sheet of paper from his coat with great theatricality. "I have here our contract." Alem said as much. "It obliges you to provide all the marble that you can produce to my company, at a rate that we agreed many years ago." Alem translated this, too. "And you have honoured this contract without fail, in a manner that does you and your people great credit, even though you could have received more—much more—for your marble by renegotiating or simply selling your marble to the Makrana buyers."

Alem said all this in increasingly awkward speech. This was a sentiment far more delicate than anything Rip had asked him to communicate before.

"Today, Rajmata Rajmata," Rip said, standing up, the contract in his hands. "I release you from that obligation." And with that, he tore the contract in two.

"Mister Ripley..." began Alem, aghast, but before he could say another word, Rajmata Rajmata was on her feet. She clicked open her new walking stick, and in a single motion she slit the throat of Ripley Standish.

∾

IT WAS ONLY a few days before word of the death of Ripley Standish reached Jaipur, but Brother Uckeridge wasn't informed until nearly Christmas. During this period the missionary's mental fortitude passed from fragile to broken and finally jabbering. In the brief time he'd lived in the compound he'd grown dependent on the tranquillity and absence of serious responsibility. There were even servants to help take care of the child. Now, his benefactor was dead—indeed, his two most generous benefactors had died in little more than a year—and he had long ago lost his taste for the challenge of finding replacements. A small amount of money remained of the generous household budget that Rip had left him, and Brother Uckeridge was decisive enough to recognise an opportunity when he saw it.

"Mister Sweet," said the monk to Handyman Sweet, as he pulled open the door of the Standish residence. "I'm so very pleased that you're here. I have very important news to impart."

"If it's about Mister Standish, I know all about it," said Handyman Sweet. "He was set upon by a horde of rebels in Auwa. Cut him into tiny pieces, they did —but mark this, Brother—they butchered him alive. He fought to the last—I heard that his severed left hand strangled one of the bastards even as he expired."

"Oh, my dear Lord." Brother Uckeridge retreated into the salon. Handyman Sweet followed and took the liberty of the drink's cabinet.

"Whisky, Brother Uckeridge? You look like you could use it."

The men helped themselves to the Standish whisky and sat regarding each other across the expanse of the broad, marble salon.

"I hear that his head is on a pike outside Fort Thakurs."

"Please, Mister Sweet, tell me no more." Brother Uckeridge took a long, slow draw of his whisky. "That is not what I wish to discuss. Handyman Sweet, I would like you to assume responsibility for this household. I've made arrangements with Mister Ripley's bank to dispose of it, but I don't wish to remain for the formalities. I'm returning to England."

"What about the boy?"

"I'm taking him with me, obviously," said Brother Uckeridge. "I shall make arrangements for him when I get to London. Doubtless there'll be relations."

Handyman Sweet contemplated the room and took a meditative sip of whisky.

"Take me with you," he said at last.

"I cannot, Mister Sweet. Someone must remain here to dispose of the household."

"Why?" said Handyman Sweet plainly. "The bank doesn't care. There's nothing left worth selling. And Brother Uckeridge, you have to take me with you—I can't stay on here. There's nothing more for me here, and if you say I'm with you, the army will pay my way too."

∽

And so, it was that Brother Uckeridge, Handyman Sweet, and a small boy were in the hold of a steamer from Bombay to Portsmouth, bypassing Africa through the recently opened Suez Canal. They shared a below-decks dormitory with a hundred sore, sweaty, sometimes seasick and constantly sleepy soldiers and adventurers, some of their family and many of the ship's crew. The boy was ill and underfed, and at some point, in the Mediterranean Sea, the household budget that Brother Uckeridge had secreted about his person went missing. He had been delirious for days, though, and suspected that he had dropped it overboard in some feverish illusion that he was relieving himself of some curse.

When they finally stumbled down the gangplank at Portsmouth, Brother Uckeridge fell to the dock and kissed it, and he wept for every moment he'd been away from England. The last act of largesse that the imperial army bestowed on Brother Uckeridge and Handyman Sweet was two, third-class train tickets to London.

At Waterloo Station, the men bade one another feeble farewells. As pleased as they were to have reached London, the milestone was made only more splendid by the end of their society with one another. In the ten and a half weeks since they had quit Jaipur together, Brother Uckeridge's anxiety and anguish had exhausted every ounce of Handyman Sweet's patience, and Handyman Sweet had given Brother Uckeridge the indelible, unassailable impression that he was an unchristian, fetid, foul-mouthed scoundrel with the personal hygiene of a bilge rat.

A penniless clergyman is never entirely without options, although for a penniless clergyman with a debt of honour to a small child they are considerably curtailed. Brother Uckeridge put himself and the boy into the charge of the Saint Gerolomo Sanctuary in Kentish Town, a refuge for orphaned boys run by the Anglican Franciscan Brotherhood. The boy thrived, Brother Uckeridge deteriorated. The other monks tolerated his disengagement from the life of the monastery because Brother Uckeridge never fully recovered from the illness of body and spirit that he'd acquired somewhere on the trip back to England.

When Brother Uckeridge died, the boy was invited to speak some words of thanks at the funeral, but he could only remember that Brother Uckeridge never beat him. By then the boy was ten years old, and it was time for him to learn a trade, so he was delivered to Clerkenwell Working Orphanage, along with what had come to be known as the book of family lore.

When he was placed at Clerkenwell it was under his real name, Theodore Standish, but he'd long before decided, all on his own, that this was an orphan name, and so he only ever called himself Teddy Tooter.

CHAPTER 14

❧

THE RETURN OF TEDDY STANDISH

"*That* settles it, Stella, you're slipping," said Jacob Nightly. "It saddens me to see it. To think I once had such great ambitions for you."

Jacob was pacing the limited space of the Reed family mausoleum and endeavouring to make the most of the space by pausing at each length and giving his beard a couple of very meaningful strokes.

"May I be frank with you, Stella?" he continued. "I had once been so enamoured of your promise that I envisaged handing over the whole lot to you, upon my retirement."

Stella sat on the stone coffin of Frederick Farnham Reed, and next to her sat Teddy. On the opposing sarcophagus, like a house of commons, was Pitty and Lucy.

"Two in a row, Stella," said Nightly. "That's got to be more than bad luck."

"Well, it ain't. There was bluebottles all over—they come to collect their share of the wine, and deliver the rest for this wedding, the bride of which, it turns out, is Isobel Merryman."

"The chief peeler's daughter?"

"Too right," said Stella. "Teddy rolled the keg out back, just like we planned, and what's there but two bobbies ready. He had to get lucky, didn't he?"

"What happened to the keg?"

"Still floating in the trench, probably."

"I waited on the water half the day, you know," complained Jacob.

"Poor sap. Next time I'll wait in the boat and you can do all the work," said Stella. "Del Daly says he's not paying you what he owes, by the by."

"I'm cursed," said Jacob, leaving his beard alone long enough to beseech the heavens. "This job would have turned more of a profit if we'd done it honestly. What's this city coming to?"

"Ain't it obvious?" said Pitty. "It's him, isn't it?"

Jacob seized his beard and observed Teddy from beneath hooded eyes.

"He does appear to be the common thread, doesn't he?"

"I ain't saying he's a nose," said Pitty. "He's too straight for that, but he ain't got the heart for it." Teddy listened to this condemnation with resignation and concentrated his attention on a spot on the floor. "Too scared and too simple." Pitty summed up the case for the prosecution.

"And where was you when Teddy and me was being chased through the drains?" asked Stella. "Or when the rozzers was on him in Bermondsey? Running away is where you was."

"You told me to," said Pitty. "Both times."

Stella cast a friendly look over the opposing benches.

"Exactly," she said, amiably. "Sometimes we make a sacrifice for each other. We take on each other's risks. That's just what Teddy done for us. Them jobs didn't go bad because of Teddy—it's down to him they didn't go a whole lot worse."

"Well, I vote Teddy goes back to the sewers," said Pitty, raising his hand theatrically.

"You vote?" said Jacob. "When did the Aldgate Apprenticeship, proprietor Jacob Nightly, become a chapter of the Reformers?"

Further discussion of the merits of democracy among criminals came to an end, then, with a knock at the door. It wasn't the secret knock, but an earnest effort to reproduce it, and hence everyone knew who it was. Jacob unlatched and opened the door.

"Come in, Sweeper."

"Good morning, Jacob. Good morning, my dear children." Sweeper lumbered into the little chapel and pushed the door closed behind him. "Bracing out there." He dropped himself weightily onto the upturned planting pot and rubbed his hands together. "You know what would dull the edge of this chill? A flagon of wine. Or perhaps a barrel. Or two, if it's not stretching a point."

"We have no wine," said Jacob. "It was a washout. We nearly got pinched."

"That is a grave disappointment," said Sweeper. "I have a lengthy list of thirsty customers."

"Come along, Mister Sweeper, and have your consolation. I have three kegs of beer in the *Maltsack*."

"It's cold outside, Mister Nightly, and what my customers want is a warm glass of dark, red wine."

"In the weeping winds of an English Spring, Mister Sweeper, your customers will take what they can get, if the price is right," said Jacob.

Sweeper shrugged. "I have a small cart and horse for the morning. I'll need a strong lad to accompany me." He cast his eye from Pitty to Teddy and then back again, and then swivelled his head rapidly back to Teddy.

"What's your name, lad?"

"Teddy."

"Teddy what?"

"Tooter."

"How very singular. I don't believe I've ever heard that surname before. Were you born with it?"

Teddy returned his gaze to the floor. "No. I chose it. I didn't like the name the orphanage gave me."

"May I be permitted to dazzle everyone here?" Sweeper stood and walked to the front of the chamber. He placed a hand over his eyes and effected to concentrate on the unknown. "The name that you believe the orphanage gave you was... Standish. Am I right?"

Teddy raised his wide eyes to meet Sweeper's. "How did you know that, sir?"

"I recognise you. I knew you as a boy and I knew your father, Ripley Standish. You resemble him something frightful. Like I was looking at the boy who became the man."

"You knew my father?" Teddy leapt to his feet. "When? Where?"

"We had many adventures together, your father and I, when we were in India. I was by his side when we were set upon by rebels in the northern territories. Nasty business. I buried him myself, that which I could find."

"Mister Sweeper, you must tell me everything you know. What of my mother?"

"I never knew your mother," said Sweeper. "She died of the fever before I met you. Last I saw of you, you had been given over to the charge of an irksome monk named Pickler or Puckridge or some such."

"Brother Uckeridge," said Teddy. "He died when I was ten."

"Uckeridge." Sweeper put his hand to his chin. "No, that doesn't sound right. No matter. So long as he's finally answering for his sins. There was much talk of his involvement when a baby girl went missing. The daughter of a close friend to your father, as it happens."

"What happened to the child?" asked Teddy.

"For certain, now that Brother Uckeridge is sharing a warm cell with Napoleon, no living man can say, but it was widely believed at the time that the child was the offering in some unholy blood ritual."

"He always seemed so… meek, I suppose," said Teddy.

"Tool of his trade."

"In any case," said Teddy. "Standish is my real name."

"It is. Did Uckeridge not leave you any documents?"

"Just a book of family lore," said Teddy. "But I lost it."

"Didn't you bring it with you from the Soap Pit?" asked Stella.

Teddy shook his head. "It all happened so fast, after we put the straw in the stove. Matron never give them my book."

"Then it'll still be at Clerkenwell, won't it?"

"Clerkenwell?" said Sweeper. "You've been to prison? Already?"

"Clerkenwell Working Orphanage," said Stella. "I was there too."

"Well, it warms my heart to see you again, my boy," said Teddy. "Have you no recollection of me? Do you recall a mango tree in your garden?"

"I don't think I'd know a mango tree if I saw one. I remember a garden, though, and climbing a tree, and then I remember a long sea voyage. I always thought it was from France."

"India," said Sweeper. "It broke my heart when I discovered that you had left, but I had much business to complete before I, too, could return.

Strange that Uckeridge recounted none of this to you."

"He was very reclusive."

"Perhaps shame finally seized upon him," said Sweeper, munificently. "And what of his fellow brothers in Christ? None of them recounted to you your pedigree?"

Teddy looked skyward for memories. "Not in detail. They said that my father was killed by revolutionaries. At some point I got that confused with the French Revolution."

"I warmly anticipate setting the record straight, Teddy Standish, but now I have many customers to disappoint in London. Pitty, won't you accompany me to the *Maltsack?*"

∽

"Thank you, Stella."

Teddy and Stella walked toward the Thames. The morning sun was only just beginning to burn the fog off the water, and the river shimmered and glared like something seen through a bottle.

"I guess we're even," she said. "You saved me at Montague and Cruikshank."

"I didn't have to make such a sacrifice, though," said Teddy. "You shouldn't have done it."

Stella grabbed Teddy's arm and stopped, causing Teddy to pivot and face her.

"What's become of Teddy Tooter?"

"What do you mean?"

"I mean where's the boy who was good at everything he did? Where's the boy who would never be an apprentice, never mind a navvy? When did you ever think you weren't worth a little sacrifice?"

Teddy turned back toward the river.

"I was ten years old, Stella," said Teddy. They had arrived at the bank, and he was scanning the breadth of the river, as though taking the measure of some endless task. "You believe a lot of things when you're ten years old. I thought my father was a French duke. I thought that naming myself after a king made me royalty."

"That's just it, though, isn't it, Teddy?" said Stella. "Turns out you was right all along."

"You heard Mister Sweeper. My father was no better than him."

"He didn't say that. He only said that they were in India together," said Stella. "And if you'll be guided by me, you won't put a lot of stock in what Sweeper tells you. There's always a grain of truth—he knows that the best lies are the fat layers worn by a slim truth—but no one who knows Sweeper believes much of what he tells them."

"You think my father was a duke?"

"No." Stella stood shoulder-to-shoulder with Teddy and together they looked at the river. "But I know that destiny has something planned for you and me."

"Like what?"

Stella took Teddy's hand.

"You said when you was rich you'd come for me, and we'd get married," she said. "I believed you. I still do. And you know what else? I always did, and now I believe it more than ever."

"I don't know why."

Stella turned to Teddy and took his other hand in hers as well.

"Teddy, don't you see what's happened? You said it wasn't luck that you was there at Montague and Cruikshank, and you were right—it was fate. Same fate as brought you to Clerkenwell. Something's always trying to keep us apart, but something better, something stronger and kinder is always bringing us back together. And whatever it is, this morning it brought Sweeper to see you, so that you can know your real name."

"What good does that do us?"

Stella smiled broadly. "I don't know that, Teddy. That's the mystery. I can tell you this, though, it's something grand and wonderful."

"You really think so, Stella?"

"How old are you now, Teddy?" asked Stella.

"Eighteen, I think, why..." Teddy's naive question was stifled and answered by Stella's lips on his.

"Teddy," said Stella, breaking the kiss with a start. "We have to get your book of family lore."

"You really think it's still at the orphanage?"

"Of course, I do."

"Why?"

"Same reason I'm here with you now, Teddy. It's waiting for you."

"It's been years. How do we get it?"

"Come to the churchyard tonight. We'll put it to the Apprenticeship," said Stella. "Jacob's a selfish, miserable, lying leg, but he's clever enough when it comes to extracting the goods."

∽

Another April tempest bore down on Aldgate that night as Teddy and Stella met in the doorway of Saint Botolph's church. Stella had dashed to scant cover beneath an oilcloth, but Teddy strolled through the sheets of rain as one who makes little distinction between dry and soaked to the skin. No gas lights stayed lit, and any moon was obscured by thick clouds, and the only light on was intermittent bursts of lightning reflecting off the slick streets. Together they dashed around the church and pushed through the door of the graveyard. They slipped and splashed through the yard to the Reed family mausoleum. Stella ignored protocol in light of the storm and pounded on the door, which snapped open.

Even on the heavy stone roof of the little clubhouse chapel the rain drummed and hummed, and then cascaded to the mud with the shout of a rushing river. Stella pushed the door closed behind them and stamped some of the rain from her clothes and hair. The interior was lit by an oil lamp which flickered scant light onto the faces of Jacob, in his position as speaker of the house, Pitty, Lucy, Emma, and Sweeper, who sat on stone coffins. They all looked wet, angry and judgemental, as though Stella and Teddy had walked in on a court in session, only to discover that they were the accused.

"You've got some bottle, coming here," said Jacob. "I can only assume, then, that you thought you'd gotten away with it."

"Away with what?" Stella fired back. "We come back because we need help."

"You need help?" exploded Jacob. "You come here asking for help? From me? From us? After what you done? Well, I'm glad of that, Stella, because it saves us the trouble of going looking for you."

"What are you rabbiting on about, you barmy old nit?"

"Maltsack," said Pitty.

"What about it?"

"It won't play, Stella," said Jacob. "You were always the clever one, but you've finally been betrayed by your best ally—chance has played you crooked."

"Is anyone not so stewed with drink they can't see a hole in a ladder?" asked Stella.

"Passions are running high," said Sweeper. "What Mister Nightly means to say is that by pure chance Pitty and I arrived at the *Maltsack* this morning just as it was towed."

"Towed? Who would tow the *Maltsack?* Who could tow it?"

"Leave it out, Stella, and let's get down to the shillings and pence. You owe me five hundred pounds." Jacob was so stirred that he was stroking his beard with alternating hands.

"What happened?" asked Stella wearily.

"The *Maltsack* has been confiscated by the canal corporation," explained Sweeper. "And sold at a no-bid auction. By the time we got there, it had been patched and towed by the new owner, carriage and contents to be disposed of at his pleasure."

"New owner? What new owner?"

"You know very well who bought my comfortable retirement for pennies to the pound, Stella," said Jacob. "Del Daly."

"Oh."

"How could you do it, Stella? You betrayed your family."

"I didn't," protested Stella.

"She didn't," said Teddy. "I did."

"No, you gulpy mug, you didn't," said Jacob. "To tell Del Daly about the barge, you'd have to know about the barge."

"Of course, I knew about your broken-down old barge," said Teddy. "You thought you were so clever, hiding your swag in a scuttle. I know every rod and pint of that canal. I probably knew about *Maltsack* before you did, and I told Del Daly about it after he caught me stealing a keg of wine. Why do you think he let me go?"

Jacob seized his beard in one hand and posed for contemplation.

"Very well then," he said. "It's you what owes me five hundred pounds."

"It's a risky business you're in. I ain't got it, so it's gone."

"Then I guess we'll cut it out of you," said Pitty. He slid from the coffin and dropped to the floor, withdrawing from his pocket a scaling knife.

"That won't save you if you follow me outside," said Teddy, turning to the door. "You like that skinny half-wit as you see him now, you'll keep him here while I leave." Teddy pulled open the door and stepped into the darkness and rain. Pitty started after him but Jacob put a hand on his shoulder.

"He's right, Pitty," said Jacob. "No good can come of pursuing into the rain a man who lifts rocks for a living."

Jacob turned his attention to Stella, whose tears were hidden by the residue of rain and the darkness of the chamber.

"I suppose I wronged you, Stella. I might have known you would never have betrayed me."

CHAPTER 15

A VIEW OF CALAIS

Mathilda Corbit had gone from strength to strength since a fateful day that she thought she remembered eight years previously. Childhood memories rarely survive into adulthood unchanged, and Matty retained the pivotal moment of her life as a snap response to the call of opportunity. The apprenticeship committee of Montague and Cruikshank were visiting the orphanage, as she recalled it, with an uncompromising mission to select the best, the most talented, and the most level-headed of the girls in training to be seamstresses. Matty believed in herself and she knew that she could rise to the top, given the chance, but such chances are not common in an average day in a working orphanage. So, when her

THE GRAVEST OF MISFORTUNES

best friend slipped and sewed her sleeves together, Matty recognised fortune's call and she leapt to answer it, snipping in a slice the thread which bound her friend to the augering needle, and Matty to the Clerkenwell Working Orphanage.

Head down and hard work soon overcame an initial unfamiliarity with the work, and as the years passed Matty grew more confident and more secure in her position and more solidly loyal to her employers. She was early to work every morning and she stayed late every night, a routine which was finally formalised in January of 1877 with a promotion to head seamstress, reporting only to Miss Steep.

On one such Friday evening in May, Matty examined every machine, swept the floor of the workshop, and then locked the front door of Montague and Cruikshank and began the long walk to her small, tidy corner of a Pimlico rooming house. She had only gone a few steps toward Waterloo Bridge, though, when she was seized by the arm and spun into the alley which led to the storm drain. In an instant, her back was to the wall and a hand was on her neck, and another held something hard and sharp to her ribs.

"Stella?" she said, on opening her eyes and recognising the notorious silk thief.

"Hello, Matty," said Stella. "I thought I owed you a visit." She released her grip and returned the weapon to the pocket of a man's coat that she wore over a worn dress. Matty, by contrast, was in a smart muslin, working-girl frock that she'd made herself.

"Stella, you got some bottle, after what you done."

"After what I done? Did I betray a friend? Did I try to get you pinched? Did I tip your plans to that Miss Steep? I think it was you done all that, Matty."

"What do you want, Stella? I don't have any money."

"I'll bet you do," said Stella. "But that's not what I want from you. You seen Teddy?"

"Teddy Tooter?"

"That's right, Teddy."

"Sometimes. He used to come round here looking for you. He works in the sewers."

"I know." Stella took Matty's arm again and led her further down the alley. "He was here that night. I hadn't seen him since the orphanage."

"I know. Why didn't you come looking for us?"

"I wanted you to have a life, Matty. As you might have reckoned by now, mine has taken a turn off the straight and narrow."

"But you don't mind robbing Montague and Cruikshank, and just in time for our biggest order of the year, too."

"I guess I'm sorry about that," said Stella, kicking sheepishly at a stone. She withdrew the sharp object from her coat pocket and took a crackling bite out of what turned out to be a shard of toffee. "Want a piece?"

"No, thank you," said Matty coolly.

"I didn't know it was Montague and Cruikshank," continued Stella. "It was just another job 'til I saw you. Did you get the dresses done?"

"Of course," said Matty casually. "You ruined a couple of bolts of silk, is all. I think the customer even paid for them."

"I'm glad, Matty, honestly. I never would have done you a bad turn knowingly."

"What's become of you, Stella? Is this what you do, now?"

"It's what I've done for years, Matty," said Stella. "I've got the knack. Have you seen Teddy since you saw me last?"

Matty shook her head. "No. He would come by once a week or so, but now I haven't seen him for a month."

"Do you know where I can find him?" asked Stella. "I've been looking for him for weeks."

"He lives underground. You'll only see him if he's looking for you. Does he know where to find you?"

"I suppose," said Stella. "But he'll never go there. You don't know where else he might go sometimes?"

"Not anymore. He used to come here, and he used to go to the orphanage, but that was because he was looking for you. Now he's found you, he's got no reason to come here or go to Clerkenwell. That just leaves one place I can think of."

"Where, Matty?"

"France."

∽

THE FOLLOWING SUNDAY WAS A WARM, early summer's day. The Thames steamed under a bright sun in a cloudless sky, and the brackish waters were high and fast with the Spring runoff. Bells rang across a city emerging into the first properly nice day of the year, and crowds crossed the bridges on foot to attend or avoid church services. The high tides chased the scavengers from the banks, and so even they were obliged to profit from the day.

For those that understand the tides, though, and how they flow and form around the arches of the bridge, and for those that, furthermore, have a dory in which to idle away a Sunday morning, a small piece of sanctuary can be carved out of the river in the middle of the maelstrom that is London in the summertime.

Teddy's little boat was consequently unmoored and pressed by the current into a wedge of still water at the base of the bridge and the bank. He sat in the sun and ate his breakfast and idly watched the other side of the river.

"I understand that you can see all the way to France from here."

Teddy knew in an instant that the voice was Stella's. Indeed, time folded suddenly in on itself in such a fashion as to give the impression that Teddy knew before she spoke that Stella would be on the bank at that moment.

"You found me."

"You made it hard enough," said Stella, as Teddy handed her aboard. "Why?"

"So, you'd be safe, of course." Teddy arranged his bread and cheese on the bench between them. "I didn't want to, but I didn't think I should come between you and your friends, not after what you did for me."

"And why do you think I did it, Teddy? Why did you kiss me if you were just going to run off?"

"You kissed me."

"And you asked me to marry you eight years ago. I could sue you for breach of promise."

Teddy laughed. "I've loved you almost since I was born, Stella. When I was ten years old, I was so sure that I could take care of you. I'd have fought a dragon for you."

"And you'd have won, I'd wager."

Teddy returned his attention to the far side of the river.

"That's when I thought there were dragons," he said. "Then I went down the mines and it was horrible. There are children down there working with broken arms, because if they say anything, they'll have no work at all. I was lucky to be so big. The Soap Pit sold my contract to the sewerage, and it weren't much better. I didn't see the sun for weeks at a time. Sometimes the miasma down there is so strong it knocks me right out, and they dock my pay for that. I have barely enough to feed myself. Everything I have you can see from where you're sitting."

"I'm sorry, Teddy. It all started with my plan to get your book."

"It don't much matter how it started, Stella, but it broke me. I don't know when it happened, but one morning I just woke up and I weren't a boy anymore. I weren't the son of a French duke or a distant cousin of King Henry. I was a navvy, and I was lucky to be that."

"We can find a way, Teddy. We were meant to."

"I thought so, too. I was so happy when I saw you again, finally. That's why I went with you to the bottlers, and what come of that? I nearly cost you everything you have."

"It's not much to lose, you can trust me on that."

"But it's more than I can give you, Stella. That's why I ran away."

"I understand, Teddy, and I only love you more for it," said Stella. She stood gingerly and stepped over the picnic and sat beside Teddy. "And you're not wrong. There's not a lot of luck for people like us, and when it is it's bad. But that's a good thing, Teddy. Bad luck makes you smarter. It makes you know what you want."

Teddy turned his attention to Stella's enthusiastic eyes.

"You said that the day I met you."

"Did I?" said Stella. "Sounds like something I'd say. And it's how we're going to work it, Teddy."

"Work what?"

Stella fixed a bemused eye on Teddy's face, and again kissed him, long and softly.

"That," she said when the kiss finally broke. "You up for it?"

"Whatever it is… yes." Teddy kissed Stella again. "What is it?"

"Your book of family lore. I figured out how we can get it from the orphanage."

"How?"

"We ask for it." Stella popped a knot of bread in her mouth. "I was trying to figure out some clever ruse as to how we might get it. Maybe dress up as a nun or blag about looking for apprentices for Montague and Cruikshank."

"That'd never work. Matron and the sisters are all still there. They'd remember us."

"Probably," said Stella. "That's what made me think of the obvious—the book is yours. They'll remember you and give it to you, just because you ask for it. Think you can manage that?"

"Of course," said Teddy. "I'm good at everything I do."

∽

THE PRISON BELL PEELED TWICE. Sister Margaret unlocked the front door of the Clerkenwell Working Orphanage and looked out upon a blessed day. The sun splashed onto the courtyard, rendering the prison walls and the cobbled ground into something more like a Roman piazza than a storehouse for the underprivileged. She glanced back into the darkened hall and gave herself pretext to enjoy a moment of good weather—she'd give thanks for it.

She walked deliberately slowly across the yard. It was empty but for a young couple at the door of the church, and without knowing why, Sister Margaret's thoughts raced across time to a cold February evening fifteen years ago, when she found a feverish child tied to the door of the church and standing in that very spot. The couple smiled timidly as she approached, and all manner of conjecture came to Sister Margaret—was the couple in trouble? Did they need to marry? Did they have a child that they needed to give over to the orphanage? And yet, again without knowing why, she knew that it was none of these things.

"Hello Sister Margaret," said Stella, as the nun arrived at the door of the church.

"Stella." Sister Margaret spoke flatly and without emotion, but her heart thrilled to know that Stella was still alive. "Stella Mallory."

"Yes, sister," said Stella. "And do you remember Teddy Tooter?"

"Is that you, Teddy?" asked Sister Margaret. "You've grown."

"I'm a navvy, sister," said Teddy, as though that explained his size.

"I'm happy to hear it," said the nun. "You were sent to the mines, if I recall."

"I was too big. They sent me back."

"Are you two… are you together?"

"Only in the most Christian way, sister," explained Stella. "We only found each other again recently."

"I had a premonition... when that man came."

"Man? What man?" asked Stella, with foreboding in her heart but not in her voice.

"Your employer," said the sister to Teddy. "He said that you were apprenticing with him, and he came to collect your valuables. Did they get to you?"

"My valuables?" asked Teddy. "You mean, my book?"

"Yes, that's right. It's an old album of documents and maps."

"And you give it to this man, sister?"

"Oh, dear, should we not have?"

"No, sister," said Stella. "That man was acting in his own interests. Did he tell you his name?"

"Yes," said Sister Margaret. "He said that his name was Sweeper."

CHAPTER 16

THE VALUE OF A GOOD BOOK

The character of Fleet Street as the geographic centre of the world's publishing industry was in its full flower at the time and encompassed everything from daily newspapers, with a circulation numbering in the hundreds of thousands, to small, family bookbinders.

One such traditional enterprise, Lovett and Son, was operated by the surviving "and Son", a Mister Henry Lovett. Mister Lovett's business was not so much seasonal as infrequent. Should a title made popular by the reading classes be elevated—say it comes to be known that a member of the royal household enjoyed the book—then a few hundred hand-bound copies might be commissioned by the publisher.

Between such windfalls, Mister Lovett contented himself with the restoration or, in a pinch, the reading of, existing books. This was a busy time, the result of a serialised bildungsroman having been mentioned in Hansard, and Mister Lovett had a very lucrative four hundred books that needed binding, to be delivered a hundred at a time, every two weeks until August. As was his practice, he had engaged "apprentices" for the brief cutting period and, that done, he arrived at his shop the following day to do the precision work himself. That morning he discovered, to his dismay, that every single square of goatskin leather was gone. Mister Lovett stood behind the counter of his shop, staring at the empty worktable, deliberating between the value of weeping or throwing something through the window.

"Mister Lovett, I presume."

Mister Lovett looked toward the door to see a large man, or at any rate, a man who wore so many layers that it was difficult to tell where his clothes stopped and he started, pointing a walking stick at the hand-painted glass, reading backwards from the inside, "Lovett and Son".

"I am not yet open for trade," managed Mister Lovett.

"I don't imagine you are," said the immense man, with a smile. "And you won't soon be, either, I fancy."

"And why should you fancy that, might I ask, sir?"

"Idle speculation on my part—pay it no mind," said the man. "Permit me to introduce myself. My name is Sweeper, and my trade is the recovery and reapplication of fine skins and fabrics. I have recently come into possession of some most excellent goatskin, already cut to measure for the binding of books about, say, this big." Sweeper held up his hands to form a rectangle.

"You've nicked my leather."

"Nicked?" said Sweeper. "You have me at a disadvantage, sir. What is this 'nicked'?"

"Give it back. Give it back now, or I'll have the police on you."

"The police, sir? I doubt if the police would have much interest in a man pursuing an honest trade. It may well be that those who sold me this leather acquired it in some questionable fashion, but I ask you, should my business suffer for the sins of others?

No, I think not, and I expect the police won't, neither."

Mister Lovett squinted poison at Sweeper, but then glanced back at the empty working surface.

"How much?" he asked.

"A snip, sir, a mere token."

"How much."

"Ha'penny a piece."

"Ha'penny? For my own leather?"

"Already cut to size, I remind you," said Sweeper.

During the brief pause while Mister Lovett calculated the new profit margin on his books, another voice joined the debate from the doorway.

"That's just the point though, isn't it?"

The counterpoint came from a pretty girl standing next to a broad-shouldered young man, standing in the sunny doorway like mismatched bookends.

"Stella. Teddy. How very pleasant," said Sweeper. "I'll be very pleased to have your company the moment I've concluded my business with Mister Lovett here."

"You give this cheap fence a ha'penny a piece for your own leather, you deserve what you got coming," said Stella to Mister Lovett.

"I fear that I have little choice."

"There you go, Stella, he has little choice," said Sweeper. "Mister Lovett here is a level-headed man of affairs, who knows a good deal when he sees one."

"He don't have much choice either, does he, Mister Lovett," argued Stella. "Who else is he going to sell four hundred pieces of custom-cut leather to?"

"Say, that's true," said Lovett. "I'll give you a shilling for the lot."

"A shilling, sir? I'm insulted. I paid fourteen shillings, in all."

"A shilling," repeated Mister Lovett. "If it's all here—every square—before this noon."

~

"I SHALL BRING suit against you, Stella, for restraint of trade," said Sweeper, once he, Stella, and Teddy were back on the bustling street.

"Only barristers you know are as crooked as you are," said Stella. "Give us back the book."

"What book?"

"Teddy's book," said Stella. "The book what you got from the orphanage."

"Ah, that book. I regret, I cannot. It's already spoken for."

"Spoken for?" said Teddy. "You can't sell it to someone else. It's mine."

"Then the orphanage shouldn't have given it to me. For all you know they might have destroyed it had I not intervened."

"That's it…" Teddy took a handful of Sweeper's layers and raised his fist.

"Stop it, Teddy," said Stella. "Not here, and not yet, anyway. Who are you selling it to, Sweeper?"

"The buyer wishes to remain anonymous."

"How much are you getting for it?"

"More than you can afford, I assure you."

"How much?"

"Five hundred pounds."

"Five hundred pounds?" said Teddy. "That's your game, is it? Nick something from someone and then sell it back to him for more than he has."

"Not in this instance, no," said Sweeper. "In this case, I'm selling it to someone else."

"Why's someone paying you five hundred pounds for Teddy's book of family lore?" asked Stella.

"I cannot say. Perhaps he is a collector of Indian artefacts."

"Sweeper, you give us back that book, or we'll follow you wherever you go," warned Stella. "That bookbinder's just the beginning. You won't make another sale in London."

"I would appreciate the company, Stella, but I'm giving up the fencing trade. With the proceeds from Teddy's book, I mean to set myself up in legitimate business. Now, thanks to you, I have a pressing task to attend to, so unless you'd care to help me deliver a hundredweight of leather, I will wish you good day."

Sweeper disappeared into the dense crowd of Fleet Street, and Stella pulled Teddy into the courtyard of the printers' guild.

"You should have let me hit him, Stella."

"It wouldn't have helped. There's no hiding savage enough that would make that man give up five hundred pounds, but that's the good news, isn't it?"

"Which bit of this is meant to be good? Where am I going to get five hundred pounds?"

"We can't, obviously, but someone can, which means that your book is worth at least that much."

Teddy leaned against a Corinthian column and looked skyward for truth.

"Why?"

"Maybe you really are royalty, Teddy."

∽

"Look who's finally come home." Jacob Nightly stood back, drawing the door of the mausoleum open. Stella stepped in.

"I've been busy," she said. "And I'm still busy, but I need help."

"You got us a caper, Stella?" asked Pitty. He and Lucy and Emma and a scattering of idle urchins were sitting in chambers on the coffins.

"Not really, no, but I need your help all the same. Has anyone seen Sweeper?"

"Since when?" asked Jacob.

"Today."

"No, why?"

"He's got something belongs to a friend of mine, and I need your help getting it back."

"Sweeper's a duffer, Stella. He doesn't give swag back, he sells it back."

"This is different."

"Who's the friend, Stella?" asked Pitty, with the air of a prosecuting counsel.

"It's Teddy, but you have to hear me out…"

Jacob pulled open the door of the chapel.

"No, Stella, we don't. That bloke sold us all out, you included."

"No, he didn't," protested Stella. "I did."

A silence deeper than the grave descended on the little parliament chamber while the representatives processed this new information.

"No, you never," concluded Pitty. "You're saying that now to protect that pucker of yours."

"It's the truth. Del Daly caught onto us at the bottlers, and we was surrounded by peelers in that trench. There was no way out. Del Daly said he'd let us go if we indemnified him."

"What does that mean?" asked Pitty.

"It means protect him against us, forever," explained Jacob.

"That's right. I didn't know what he was going to do, I thought he just wanted the goods on us so we couldn't never clip him again. So, I told him. I told him about the apprenticeships, about Sweeper, and I told him about the barge, as a matter of pure by-the-by."

"And he used his big smoke insights to buy it at a no-bid auction, patch it up, and tow it away, with all my swag inside." Jacob was holding his beard, now, as though he feared it might attempt an escape.

"I'm sorry, Jacob, I truly am, but if you think I sold you out deliberately, then I guess we never knew each other."

"What you intended doesn't matter, Stella," said Jacob. "All that matters is what you've done to us. All of us. There are rules. Traditions."

Stella walked to the head of the chamber. "Traditions? Rules? For a gang of thieves? There's just the one tradition, and that's that we look out for each other. The Apprenticeship's the only family I've ever had, from when I was nine years old and Pitty tried to steal my boots on the embankment—because he thought I was dead. How's that for rules? Twick's in gaol now, and he'll be there for six more months, when he could be out by now if he'd told the court where we got them forged notes, but then you'd be in gaol too, wouldn't you? Pitty and Lucy are here now because Teddy and me stayed behind when we saw them peelers."

"That's part of the tradition," said Jacob, flatly.

"That's the only tradition," said Stella. "The only one that matters. If it don't matter to you, then I guess I'm done with you. I guess I'm an orphan again."

"Wнат are you doing here?" said Del Daly at the sight of Stella and Teddy outside his bottling plant as he was locking up for the evening. "I beg your pardon, please allow me to rephrase that—what *the devil* are you doing here?"

"We come to ask for your help," said Stella.

Daly stared at the young couple, by all appearances frozen in time, but for the occasional blink of his eyes.

"You've come to ask me for help," he said. "After trying to steal from me."

"You made out all right out of it," said Stella.

"That's my trade," said Daly. "I buy and sell that upon which a debt is owed. That hulk in the Limehouse Cut was a hazard to navigation, abandoned by its owners, and hence by default property of the state."

"Fine by me," said Stella. "As I see it, though, you owe me. I'm here to collect."

Daly bestowed a hollow, avuncular smile on Stella and Teddy.

"Very well," he said. "Suppose I agreed to help you. What would you have me do?"

"Nothing, just… you know things, don't you?"

"Many things, yes."

"About the law, I mean. And how to use it to get what you want."

"I resent that," said Daly. "I'm as much a subject to the law as anyone. Perhaps I navigate it with greater facility than some, but I can say that I at the very least stay within it."

"That's just it," said Stella. "Someone's got something that belongs to Teddy, and we want to know how to get it back."

"You belong to a gang of notorious criminals," observed Daly. "I would assume that you would just crack him over the head with a cosh and take it."

"That's not an option, in this case, I don't suppose," said Stella, without conviction.

"Who is this person, and what is it that he's taken from you?"

"That bloke I told you about, Sweeper, the duffer for the Apprenticeship," said Stella. "He's got a book of family lore that belonged to Teddy's father, and now it belongs to Teddy. Sweeper went to the orphanage, where it was held for him, and he took it."

"Why?"

"He's going to sell it to someone," said Teddy.

"He's going to sell your book of family lore?" said Daly. "How much can it be worth?"

"Five hundred pounds," answered Teddy.

"For a book of family lore? I find that difficult to believe. What's in it?"

"That's just it," said Stella. "Teddy don't remember. Just some documents and maps and things. But it's his, no matter what it's worth, that's the law."

"There's what the law says and what the law does," said Daly. "And furthermore, there's what the law will do for those without means."

"For the poor, you mean," said Stella.

"To put a word on it, yes. I, on the other hand, have means. So, the question is, what's my share?"

Teddy and Stella shared a meaningful glance.

"We don't know," said Stella. "We don't even know what's in it, or why it's worth so much."

Daly's scrutiny shifted from Stella, to Teddy, and back again. He pushed up the sleeves of his coat and the shirt underneath, and he crossed his arms.

"Against my better judgement," he said. "I'll see if there's anything that can be done. Suppose my friends among the police were looking for this Sweeper fellow, where might they find him?"

CHAPTER 17

A SCOUNDREL IN HIS NATURAL HABITAT

The Docker's Arms in Shadwell, formerly the Horsemen, formerly the Shatfleet Tavern, formerly a common bawdy house, was a working man's pub into which few working men ever strayed. Its proximity to the Shadwell Basin and convenience to the men who worked there was counterbalanced by the bright and amiable White Hart directly across the street, and the Docker's reputation for low dealing. The management of the Docker's long ago abandoned any effort to compete with the White Hart, and instead embraced its dodgy reputation and catered to the consequent clientele with cloaked windows, low ceilings, dusty, sticky surfaces, unwashed tankards, and cheap, usually black market, beer and spirits. That, in addition to the Docker's East End location, rear exit, and access to any number of discreet landing points for contraband, made for a very welcoming atmosphere for Sweeper and men like him to meet and discuss terms.

The barman and proprietor, Lyle Pilky, knew his customers and he knew what they liked, and what Sweeper liked was fair warning. So, when a formally dressed gentleman of a pedigree never seen inside the Docker's paced deliberately in and up to the bar one early evening and asked to be directed to a Mister Sweeper, Pilky screwed up his brow as though trying to recall such a name.

"Mister Sweeper, you say, sir?" said Pilky, with a booming baritone. Sweeper occupied a corner table in the low, dark, smoky lounge, and he heard and understood Pilky's evasiveness. He glanced imperceptibly toward the bar and saw what the barman had seen—a man that neither of them recognised and who could only bring sad tidings. With the subtlest of gestures, Sweeper indicated a "no" to Pilky, who in turn said to the gentleman, "I don't believe I know anyone of that name, sir."

The gentleman, however, wasn't to be put off. What's more, he had the talent and training to spot a flam when he saw one, no matter how subtle, and he followed the barman's eye into the lounge, all the way to the corner table.

"Thank you," said the man. "Make mine a bitter." He accepted and paid for his drink and then walked straight to Sweeper's table and took the seat across from him.

"Mister Sweeper," said the man. "My name is Daly."

"How may I be of service, Mister Daly?"

Daly took a long draw on his beer. "That… is appalling."

"I could have advised you to only order that which comes out of a bottle here."

"I'll keep it in mind for the next time I meet a scoundrel in his natural habitat."

"If you came here to insult me, sir, you may now take your leave," said Sweeper, effecting to be distracted by his glass of whisky. "You have accomplished your goal."

THE GRAVEST OF MISFORTUNES

"That was not the principal reason for my visit. It is merely a... desirable dividend, if you will," said Daly. "You are familiar, I understand, with a bright young lady who calls herself Stella, and a powerfully built young man known as Teddy."

"You are free to believe what you wish, Mister Daly." Sweeper's demeanour was unshaken, but he glanced at the dusty purple curtain next to his table. To sweep aside the curtain and flee to the alley behind the pub would be, he knew from repeated instances of doing exactly that, the work of seconds.

"Most considerate, Mister Sweeper, for I go on to believe that you are in possession of a book, belonging to the boy."

"I regret, sir," said Sweeper, his attention drawn by a mote of dust on one of his many sleeves, "that your fancies fail to capture my interest."

"Indeed," conceded Daly. "Let me try another tack. You know who I am, can we agree on that?"

Sweeper considered this and, finally, nodded. "Agreed."

"Then you know that I was recently one of your intended victims, and that I not only bested you in your own arena, but I came out considerably the better man."

"That, sir, is a matter of opinion," contested Sweeper, but he was now giving Daly his full attention.

"But do you know why I so handily foiled you and your accomplices, Mister Sweeper?"

"Of course," said Sweeper, allowing the wound to his professional pride to influence his tone. "You profited from an uneven advantage, sir—a venal relationship with the police."

Daly sat back and smiled, and he observed Sweeper from a position of advantage.

"What is it that you want, Mister Daly?"

"I want to help," said Daly. "You mean to sell the book for five hundred pounds. I suspect it's worth a good deal more than that."

"Not to you it's not, nor to me."

"No, that is what I presumed," said Daly. "I understand that the book is composed of documents and maps from India. Doubtless of immense value to those who know how to profit from them, nearly worthless to those who don't."

"Exactly. Five hundred pounds is the most I can hope to realise from my client."

"And this is where I propose to be of value to you," said Daly, leaning forward and putting both elbows on the table. "I will be your second client."

"I trust there's more to this proposal."

"Not very much, no," said Daly. "It's what I do—I purchase goods at auction. I understand what might be called the vigour of the auction house. Spirits run high. It is why auctions exist—to extract the most that the market will bear."

"You would bid against my client."

"I would."

"I appreciate that you're a successful businessman, Mister Daly, but I believe that your plan has a fatal flaw."

"What if I were to win the auction."

"Precisely," said Sweeper. "Unless you plan to match the price bid, I lose a customer and five hundred pounds."

"If your customer abandons the auction—a highly improbable contingency—then I will buy the book from you for the originally agreed price—five hundred pounds. You can't lose either way. Anything your customer pays you over five hundred pounds, thanks to my intervention, you divide with me. Should he pay you a thousand pounds, you give me two hundred and fifty and you keep seven hundred and fifty for yourself. What do you think of that?"

"What would you want with the book?" asked Sweeper, although a practised hand like Daly could tell that he was already mentally spending the additional two hundred and fifty pounds.

"You said yourself that it's worthless unless you know what to do with it."

"Indeed, but we already know that it's worth five hundred pounds to your client," said Daly. "I would seek him out and sell it to him and, in the worst of all possible eventualities, I would cover my loss."

Sweeper leaned away from the table, taking his whisky with him.

"There may be something to what you propose," he said. "In truth, I know that this book is worth a good deal more to my client than five hundred pounds, but in turn he knows that it has little value to anyone else."

"Has your client some expertise in the area of Indian property and investments?"

"None whatever," said Sweeper. "His interest is purely legal."

"Then I shall effect such an expertise and take the position that I can exploit the book to such a degree that I'm willing to pay up to two thousand pounds."

"As much as that?"

"Why not?" asked Daly. "It's fool proof."

Sweeper glanced around the otherwise empty lounge, then raised his glass in a toast.

"To low cunning, Mister Daly."

Daly raised his tankard and tapped it to Sweeper's glass but didn't drink.

"You'll forgive me if I don't drink this… whatever this is," he said.

"Indeed, Mister Sweeper, I will take the opportunity to propose a business arrangement with the landlord."

"You are dogged, Mister Daly," said Sweeper. "I respect that."

"Only in business, Mister Sweeper. I never miss an opportunity to turn a profit."

CHAPTER 18

MONSOON SEASON

Monsoon season came to Jaipur exactly on schedule on the 1st of July 1862. Matthew Blythe and Ripley Standish had anticipated the eventuality and were safely at home by the night before. Handyman Sweet had been to their houses and secured all the windows, shutters and non-essential doors, and had confirmed the good working order of the gutters.

Bethany was eighteen months old, and her only playmate was Teddy Standish, whose name she had yet to learn. He was two and a half years old. They were on the cool marble floor of her room, playing a somewhat unstructured game of handing objects, such as marbles, pinafores and building blocks, to one another in a lively if somewhat circular commerce. The game didn't progress, but the children enjoyed it enormously, and Bethany, in particular, would laugh with abandon when Teddy would pass an object behind his back, only to reproduce it a moment later in the other hand.

The rain was already beating against the last shutters in the Blythe household as Handyman Sweet secured them with wire. This was Bethany's room, and so he took extra care with both the window and shutters, adhering the wire to the locking mechanism, and then training it discreetly between the slats and feeding it outside. He glanced around and determined that the only witnesses were a toddler and an infant, and he gave the wire a pull. He was rewarded with a subtle but satisfying "click" and the shutters were unlocked.

"Are you about done, Mister Sweet?" The voice from the door gave Handyman Sweet a start.

"Just double-checking little Bethany's room," said Handyman Sweet. "We don't want her carried off in a flood."

"Come along, Theo," said Rip to his son, officially Theodore Standish but known to his father and his father's friends as Theo, and to the future as Teddy.

Rip slipped his hands beneath his son's arms and Teddy, in turn, slipped his hands beneath Bethany's.

"No, sorry, Theo," said Rip. "Bethany has to stay here tonight, but you can see her again tomorrow." And as he separated the children, they raised a chorus of agonies and wailed against life's injustices.

∽

Handyman Sweet was usually harried and intimidated by the crowds and activity of the Tripolia Bazar, a busy street and vibrant market radiating in three directions from the Tripolia gate, the paradoxically private entrance to the City Palace. Today, Handyman Sweet welcomed the attendant anonymity. Everyone either rushed, single-mindedly, from doorway to doorway, or they hid beneath umbrellas and behind screens of rain. Handyman Sweet held his umbrella low as he ambled up the street on the extreme opposite side to the palace, trying but failing to affect an interest in mangos, silks and spices.

Where the crowd thinned and the bazar grew darker, Handyman Sweet crossed the street and pressed himself between two shops. The rain on the tin roofs was like a drumbeat and they both evacuated directly onto his umbrella. The sides of the shops had no windows and only one of them had a door. Handyman Sweet knocked lightly, then harder when there was no answer. Finally, the door opened a crack, a short man placed a big, brown eye in view, blinked, and then pulled the door open far enough to allow Handyman Sweet to enter. The door was swiftly closed behind him.

Inside the rain was even louder than it was outside, but it was dry and warm. The heat and only light was a fire in an iron stove. During business hours the shop was a cutler, selling and sharpening knives, all manner of which were on display on the walls. A screen blocked the front of the shop from a lounge formed of embroidered cushions, on which sat a stocky, local man with only one eye and a scarred ear. The respective injuries didn't appear to have been caused by the same incident. The short man at the door was the opposite—trim, well-dressed and clipped. Both men, however, shared a countenance of impatience. On a large cushion next to the stocky man was Bethany Blythe. She cried distractedly, as though she'd been doing so all day and was bored with the pastime, and in any case, her cries were drowned out by the rain.

"Have you any news?" asked the clipped man at the door.

"Have you anything to drink, Alem?"

Alem went to the stove on which was simmering a copper kettle.

"I meant something to counter the effects of the rain," corrected Handyman Sweet.

"Many find hot tea suitable to the requirement," said Alem, nevertheless pouring himself a small ceramic cup. "Is there any news?"

"They have the money," said Handyman Sweet. "You just need to go and get it."

"They have the money?" said the stocky man, rocking to his feet. "They are amazing, the British. They can have twenty-five thousand rupees from their bank, just for the asking."

"Just as I said, Vish," said Handyman Sweet. "If that's really all there is, Alem, I believe I will accept a cup of tea."

Alem shrugged in the direction of the stove and Handyman Sweet served himself a cup.

"Too easy," said Vish. "We should have asked for more. I said that we should have asked for more. Twenty-five thousand each."

"Do not be absurd, Vish," said Alem. "Twenty-five thousand is ample. Had we asked for more the police would surely have become involved."

"Caution," spat Vish. "Caution in all things, but for the taking of a British baby. For that, Vish can risk his life. I want more."

"No, Vish, the plan has worked. Let us not upset the balance at this late stage. By tomorrow, we will have returned the baby, and divided the ransom."

"No," said Vish. A vile smile stretched itself across his face, twisting madly as it met the scar on his left cheek. "Tomorrow we will collect the ransom and demand the remainder—fifty-thousand rupees."

A gust of wind swept a carpet of rain across the roof of the shop, striking it as though with a hammer, and the tin roof echoed and shook.

"They won't pay it," said Alem. "If we ask for more, they will assume that we will only continue to ask for more, and they will cease to believe us."

"No, they will not cease to believe us," corrected Vish, "because with the note, demanding fifty-thousand rupees, we will send proof that we mean what we say." As he spoke, Vish was browsing a display of knives on the wall. He selected a heavy cleaver and tested its blade on his finger.

"Alem, you must calm him down," said Handyman Sweet.

"Vish, we agreed this plan. We discussed every detail."

Vish looked up from the blade. "The plan is changed." He approached the baby, who in that moment ceased crying and looked the kidnapper in the eye.

"Vish, no," ordered Alem, but Vish was now crouching over Bethany and reaching for her foot.

The other two men cast one another a frenzied look, and then as one tackled Vish and held his arms away from the child.

"Let me go," said Vish, with unnerving calm. "Or I'll have the entire ransom for myself." He easily tore his arm from Alem's grip and slashed at Handyman Sweet who, in dodging the blade, fell back against the door. Vish levelled the knife at both men and smiled his twisted, menacing smile. He snorted, then turned back to Bethany. He went down on one knee and took hold of her right leg. He turned his twisted grin to the baby's tranquil face and then threw his head back as a stabbing pain shot through his body, starting from somewhere below his ribs.

Arched backward but still nimble, Vish stood and turned to face the desperate countenance of Alem.

"You should have remained cautious, Alem," said Vish, and approached the smaller man. Handyman Sweet reached for the first weapon to hand—a pair of sewing shears—and slashed at Vish from a distance. Thusly distracted, he was momentarily defenceless as Alem pulled a machete from the wall and in the same movement brought it down on Vish's head like an axe. The blade sunk deeply into the kidnapper's skull. He stood for a moment, unseeing eyes staring straight ahead, and then he collapsed onto himself. Blood issued onto the floor like a split wine barrel.

"Dear God, Alem, what have you done?" said Handyman Sweet.

Alem didn't reply. He stared aghast at the corpse of his former colleague.

"We must get out of here."

"Yes," said Handyman Sweet, as though recovering from a dream. "Yes. Goodbye, Alem, and good luck." He turned to the door.

"No, we cannot just leave, we must do something about the baby."

"Why? When they find Vish they'll make the obvious assumption—he kidnapped the baby alone."

"Alone? Mister Sweet, who do you think the police will think killed him, then?"

"Oh, yes," said Handyman Sweet. "Of course. What will we do?"

"We must get rid of the child."

"No, Alem, that's where I draw the line. I'm not killing a child."

"We will not kill the child, Mister Sweet, but she cannot remain here, and we can no longer risk being connected to this affair."

They both stared at Bethany. Finally, Handyman Sweet said, quietly and conclusively, "Baby market."

"What is that you say?"

"Baby market. We'll sell her onto the baby market."

"How much could we possibly get?"

"It doesn't matter. Five hundred rupees, perhaps."

Alem surveyed the turmoil. Bethany squirmed on a cushion his accomplice's blood was flooding the floor.

"From five thousand rupees to five hundred," he said glumly.

"It's better than a noose," said Handyman Sweet. "Vish will be found murdered in his own shop. The child will be transported somewhere far away—Malaya, or Singapore. Within a month she'll have a new name. And we'll have no further connection to this cursed affair."

CHAPTER 19

THE VIGOUR OF THE AUCTION

*E*xactly fifteen years later, on the 1st of July 1877, it rained again. The torrents and thunder, the coincidence of the date, and the furtive nature of the evening's business, all served to remind Handyman Sweet, now calling himself Sweeper, where he was fifteen years previously. He wondered what became of the girl and, as he generally did when he thought of Bethany Blythe, he wished her well, as though that in some fashion absolved him.

As he'd done fifteen years before, Sweeper remained aloof and anonymous under his umbrella in the pouring rain. He lingered under the jolly gas lights of the White Hart, and he observed the entrance of the Docker's Arms. It was a Sunday, a quiet day for the Docker's, and by Sweeper's estimation there were no customers at all. And so, he lingered on.

Finally, the gaunt, hesitant figure of Max Blythe cast a distinctive shadow against the screen of rain. He edged his way along the outside of the Docker's, looking this way and that, and holding his umbrella low. Then, in a decisive moment, he dashed inside the pub, shook his umbrella behind him, and disappeared into the darkness. Five minutes later, the squat, bold silhouette of Del Daly gambolled down the street and, without stopping to cast any conspiratorial looks up and down the street, he too went into the pub. Sweeper crossed the street, a leather satchel hugged to his chest beneath several layers of coats.

Sweeper exchanged a glance with Pilky, who poured and passed over a glass of whisky.

"Best let me have the bottle," said Sweeper, with a gesture toward the corner table, at which sat a smiling Del Daly and a baffled and offended Max Blythe. Clearly, Daly had already introduced himself, and equally clearly Blythe was not charmed. Blythe had a full glass of whisky. Daly had emptied his.

"Good evening, gentlemen," said Sweeper. He dragged a chair from another table and positioned himself between the bidders.

"What is the meaning of this, Sweeper? Who is this man?" asked Blythe, with a discreet but outraged whisper that sounded more like a hoarse shout.

"This is Mister Daly," said Sweeper. "I regret that I couldn't inform you of his involvement, but you see…" Sweeper caught Daly's eye with a suspicious squint. "But perhaps Mister Daly has already explained his interest in this affair."

"He has not. He has only very rudely introduced himself and demanded to know my name."

"Very well, Mister Daly, this is Max Blythe," said Sweeper. "Mister Blythe, I had no choice but allow Mister Daly to… to participate… in tonight's proceedings."

"Participate? In what manner will Mister Daly be participating?"

"As a bidder, of course," said Daly.

Blythe fixed a venomous glare on Sweeper. "A bidder? I understood that we had fixed a price."

"Oh, we had, Mister Blythe, and anyone who knows me will tell you, sir, I'm a man of my word, but Mister Daly, here, he has…" Sweeper looked into his glass for inspiration. "He has a claim."

"A claim?"

"That's right," said Sweeper, either happy with the direction this fib was taking him or committed to it regardless of quality.

"You see, Mister Daly helped me recover the book. It was him found out where it was, you see, and him what fronted me some of the brass to buy it."

"You bought it." Blythe said this as though it was self-evidently false to all present. "I don't see how this concerns me. You are welcome to compensate Mister Daly as you see fit, out of the price we agreed."

"Mister Daly doesn't wish to be compensated, does he, Mister Daly?"

"I do not," said Daly. He poured himself another glass of whisky from the bottle that Sweeper had brought to the table. "What I want is the book. Mister Sweeper, however, explained to me that it was already spoken for, and so I proposed that we settle the question like gentlemen—with an auction."

"An auction," said Blythe, with much the same tone with which he'd said 'You bought it' only moments before. "I think not. The book is mine. It's of no value to you."

"That's where I think you may be wrong, Mister Blythe," said Daly. "May I see the book, Mister Sweeper?"

Sweeper glanced again around the empty barroom. It remained dark and smoky and, but for the three men, empty. He withdrew the satchel onto this lap, opened it, and took out a heavy album. It was leather-bound and had once upon a time had gold-painted lettering across the cover. It had likely been a handsome volume, but now it was cracked and withered, and bits of dried leather fell away when Sweeper placed it on the table.

Daly opened the book at random. Each page was a thick, yellowing sheet of linen-weaved paper, on which was affixed, in one manner or another, a document or an envelope containing one. Daly unfolded a map away from the current page.

"This, for instance," he said. "I believe this to be the location of buried treasure."

"Nonsense," said Blythe. "These are old, obsolete documents, of no interest to anyone but myself, for reasons of my own."

"What do you make of that, then?" said Daly, pointing to a fading circle made in ink.

"It's a location on a map," observed Blythe. "Not every location marked on every map designates buried treasure."

"You have your interpretation, I have mine."

Blythe slammed the book shut.

"Mister Sweeper, we had an arrangement. However, if you insist on playing me crooked, then I concede. I will give you another hundred pounds."

Daly smiled, took another swallow of whisky, and rubbed his hands together. "Six hundred and fifty."

"No, we are not bidding, six hundred is my final offer."

"Then I'm afraid that Mister Daly wins the auction," said Sweeper.

"Ha HA!" gloated Daly and reached for the book.

"Very well, seven hundred."

"Seven fifty."

"Eight hundred, not a penny more."

Daly paused and put his hands on the table by the fingertips. "Not a penny more?"

"Not a pen…" Blythe began to shout when all three men were distracted by movement at the entrance. Pilky came out from the bar to receive a shipment of beer, arriving in the form of three large kegs, rolling through the entrance.

"Not a penny more," whispered Blythe.

"Very well, then," said Daly. "Eight hundred and one."

"This is absurd. I refuse to participate in this farce."

"Mister Blythe," said Daly, his voice and face hard. "You will. You see, this book doesn't belong to you nor me nor Mister Sweeper here, it belongs to a lad named Teddy Tooter, and he's asked for my help in getting it back."

"You're acting on behalf of this boy?"

Daly smiled, now, but it was a mirthless, diabolical grin, which he shared with both men.

"No, Mister Blythe, I'm not acting on anyone's behalf but my own, but I'm letting you know that you'll either bid for the book and win it or lose it like a gentleman. Or I'll stand aside and let the police act on the boy's behalf." Daly took a draw of his whisky. "Now, any raise on eight hundred and one?"

Blythe glared his disdain at both men, and then finally said, "Nine hundred."

"That's better," said Daly. "Nine fifty."

"A thousand pounds is the absolute limit, Mister Sweeper," pleaded Blythe. "And even then, I'll be forced to sell…"

Blythe had more of a case to make, but at that moment one of the boys by the bar shouted something that was meant to be "look out!" but came out as "oo-oooohh!", and his barrel bounced down the steps into the lounge, bounded off a table, knocked over a chair, and continued on unabated and in an unrelenting rush straight toward the auction. The excitement caused the second boy to lose control of his barrel and it, too, bounced into the lounge with an effect on all concerned of many more than two barrels. Sweeper dashed to the safety of the other side of the lounge, Blythe pressed himself against the wall as a keg brushed past his knees, and Daly, with boyish aplomb, leapt over a barrel as it threatened to cripple him for life.

The first barrel knocked over their table, hit the opposing wall of the lounge, and deflected back toward the middle of the room, where it collided with its brother, and the chaos was at an end.

"You clumsy ox," shouted Blythe. "You might have killed me."

"Beg pardon, sir," said the boy who'd lost control of the first barrel. "It's my first day, sir."

"I shall speak to your employer and be certain that it is your last." Blythe cast a spiteful eye over the room in general and Sweeper and Daly in particular.

"Let us conclude our business. I wish to spend no longer here than absolutely necessary." He looked toward the table, now on its side. "Where is the book?"

Sweeper looked to Daly, who looked to Blythe, who returned the look of distrust with sincere meaning.

Daly held his hands in the air, as though to show that they were empty.

"Where is it?" spat Sweeper. "Give it back." He turned to Blythe. "I'm sorry Mister Blythe. It's yours for five hundred pounds, just as we agreed."

"Then where is it?"

Again, they both looked to Daly, and then followed his gaze to the purple curtain, which had been pulled aside, revealing the hall which led to the alley—the discreet rear exit.

"After him, curse you," shouted Daly, and led the charge into the corridor.

Moments later the men were standing in a dark alley in the rain. Within moments they were soaked to the skin, and despair had overcome them.

"Doubtless you've outwitted us both, somehow, Mister Daly," said Blythe, now indifferent to the rain and cold. "I will pay you a thousand pounds for that book."

"A clever ruse, Mister Blythe," countered Daly. "It was you who staged this illusion, and very deft it was, too. I think it only fair that you give us, at the very least, the five hundred pounds that was originally agreed."

"How could I have arranged such a thing? I only learned this morning that we were to meet in this place."

Daly turned his attention to Sweeper. "This is your doing."

"You think I arranged this? Why would I do such a thing—it is my fondest wish to complete this sale."

"You buffoon," said Daly. "Of course, you didn't organise this deception—you haven't the wit to organise a game of cards. But it was you who chose this place, of all places, to do business—the one place in all of London where everyone, and most particularly Jacob Nightly and his band of miscreants, knows where to find you."

"Who is Jacob Nightly?" asked Blythe.

"Just a no good scoundrel, with no end of boys with barrels and sneak thieves at his disposal."

"There may be something to this," said Sweeper.

"Let us discuss this out of the rain," said Blythe.

"A fresh bottle, if you please, landlord," said Sweeper to Pilky, who was in that moment righting their table.

"How do we find this Jacob Nightly," asked Blythe, after steadying his nerves with a fresh dose of whisky.

"Doubtless he will find you," said Daly.

"I can only think of the graveyard," said Sweeper.

"Graveyard? What graveyard?" asked Blythe.

"Saint Botolph's. In Aldgate. It's where Nightly has his office."

"Then what are you waiting for? Go at once and recover my book," said Blythe. He stood and began to take his leave but stopped with an afterthought. "And you'd best find him before he finds me, Mister Sweeper, for I will have no hesitation to strike a deal with Mister Nightly, if he has my book."

CHAPTER 20

THE END OF THE BEGINNING

He could get no wetter, so Del Daly walked from Shadwell to Bermondsey. By the time he arrived at Shad Thames and his bottling plant, the rain had ceased and given way to a warm July midnight, with a high, bright, three-quarter moon.

Daly approached his plant from the back, next to Canute's Trench, and stopped at the rear door. Inside were muted voices, and between the door timbers, the light from a lamp flickered. The door pushed open easily and quietly. Daly peeled off his jacket and vest and hung them from a tap, and then stepped into the light of the lamp.

The two clumsy boys from the Docker's Arms were there, as was Pitty, Lucy, Jacob Nightly, Stella, and Teddy. They stood as though in conference around the corking table, passing from hand to hand a bottle of wine.

"I'm pleased to see that you've made yourselves comfortable," said Daly.

"I suppose you know what to make of all this," said Jacob, gesturing to the book of family lore which lay open before him.

"Let us have a considered look."

Daly turned the book to face him and, starting from the back, turned the pages carefully, examining the broad range of maps, contracts, deeds, and certificates. All of them were dated, in one manner or another, starting from 19th October, 1863.

"Much of this appears to encompass the legal affairs of one Ripley Standish," said Daly. "Your father, I presume," he said to Teddy.

"Is Teddy rich?" asked Stella.

"Quite possibly," said Daly. "It's unclear what became of these assets after October of 1863 when much of them were converted to bonds and shares. Prior to that, Mister Standish appears to have been part of an engineering consortium."

"Then what was the interest of Sweeper's client in the book?" asked Jacob.

"That, Mister Nightly, is the question. The assets inventoried herein amount to the tens of thousands, but the only mention of the name Blythe is a Matthew Blythe, who appears to have been a business partner to Mister Standish. However, his interest in the operation ceases at some point in 1862."

"He must believe that this gives him some claim to Teddy's inheritance," suggested Jacob.

"Possibly..." said Daly, turning the pages as he spoke, "...but I rather think it more likely that this was the object of his interest."

A certificate had been glued to the page in such a fashion that it could be unfolded away from it.

"It's a declaration of live birth, confirming the British citizenship of one Bethany Blythe, born in Jaipur, India on 2nd February, 1860, to Matthew and Faith Blythe."

Daly glanced up at the audience of intrigued faces.

"Does anyone here know of anyone of that name?"

The intrigued faces cast intrigued glances at one another, and then as one shook their heads in the negative.

"Could it be that this Blythe fellow is simply trying to find some long-lost niece?" suggested Jacob.

"I think not," said Daly. "Max Blythe didn't strike me as the sentimental kind. No, I deem it considerably more probable that his purpose was to destroy this document."

"But why?" asked Teddy. "It's my father's fortune, isn't it?"

"That which is documented here, yes," said Daly. He turned the pages now toward the present. "But what if Mister Max Blythe was protecting his claim on Matthew Blythe's estate… something caught my eye a moment ago…" Daly turned to a page fixed with faded photographs. He took one from its paper corners and examined it closely.

"You rather resemble your father, Teddy." Daly turned the photograph for the others to see. "And you, Stella, are the image of your mother.

THE GRAVEST OF MISFORTUNES

The picture was brown and badly faded at the edges, but the high-quality paper of the book of Standish family lore had protected the essential image. It depicted two couples. One of them was a slight woman and a broad-shouldered, smiling man who could be none other than Ripley Standish, and he held the hand of a small boy who, even as a toddler, already resembled Teddy. The other couple was a handsome man and a tall, patrician woman who looked so chillingly like Stella that the assembly was struck momentarily dumb.

Teddy and Stella turned slowly to gaze their amazement at each other.

"You see, Teddy," said Stella. "We weren't just always meant to be together we've always been together."

"What of our parents, Mister Daly?" asked Teddy. "Are they still in India?"

Daly shared a sympathetic look with Stella. "I think it likely that your parents are no longer with us, Teddy. You are orphans, and circumstances and thievery have conspired to deny you your legacies."

"Is there no way we can retrieve them," asked Stella. "Or is this another one of those matters in which the law only intervenes on behalf of the rich."

"Teddy's wealth, so far as I can tell, is in India," said Daly. "And yes, it will require capital to acquire it. Yours, however, I believe is in the possession of Max Blythe, and you have the key to claiming it back."

"How? What key?" asked Stella. "Surely my resemblance to my mother can be challenged by a man of means like Max Blythe."

Daly once again turned the pages of the book, back to the birth certificate.

"A most curious document," he said. "Mister and Mrs Blythe have signed their names, but, like many of what I assume are contracts, they have also affixed their fingerprints. And the child, it would appear, has borne witness with the print of her right foot."

Again, curious glances were exchanged, and the bafflement eventually settled once again on Daly.

"It is a matter of legal fact, established in India, and accepted across the empire, that finger and footprints are unique to the individual. With this document, paper, and a bottle of ink—and your right foot—we can prove unequivocally that you are Bethany Blythe."

MAX BLYTHE DISPUTED the proof of the footprint. His solicitors also disputed the signature of Matthew Blythe and Ripley Standish. They challenged the standing of documents from India in a British court. When all that failed, they endeavoured to negotiate with the solicitors representing Del Daly on behalf of Bethany Blythe, and finally, they settled on a modest stipend, to be paid retroactively, to Max Blythe, in consideration of his management of Stella's estate during the preceding fifteen years— now sixteen years, by the end of the court proceedings. This left Max Blythe, after paying his solicitors, with just over seven hundred pounds, several excellent suits of clothes, a top hat, and a membership at Pratt's. In the run up to Christmas, 1878, he was taken on as a clerk at the Holland Park Hotel.

The Aldgate Apprenticeship moved its headquarters permanently into the premises of Bermondsey Bottling, and developed a speciality in preparing young boys and girls for careers in the drinks, hospitality, and bottling trades, and Jacob Nightly managed the bottler as a showpiece of this venture.

Meanwhile, from the end of 1877 to the beginning of 1879, Del Daly and Teddy Standish were in India.

In the absence of legal challenges, Teddy's claim on his father's estate was executed much more smoothly, but so complex and diverse were the holdings that it took over a year to identify, liquidate, and transport the legacy back to London.

When Teddy returned in March of 1879, he was a rich man. So was Del Daly, for his trouble, and everyone was older and wiser. Teddy was twenty years old. Stella was nineteen, and she had moved from boarding house, to rooming house, to a rented house in the smart quarter of Marylebone. She only knew from a telegram that Teddy's ship would dock sometime that month, but she knew, possibly even before the tap on the door, that he was home.

"Mister Theodore Standish, Miss," announced Jane Thorne, formerly of the Clerkenwell Working Orphanage, and now a promising young housemaid in the employ of the newly wealthy Stella Bethany Blythe. Stella positioned herself at the window overlooking the modest damp, green, walled garden. She was in an apple-green silk dress, and her hair was woven about her head in a passable recreation of the style her mother wore in the picture of the Blythe and Standish families, now occupying the place of honour on the mantelpiece. It was the only picture in the room that meant anything to Stella, the rest had come with the house, and they only contributed to the Victorian clutter of the drawing-room.

Jane drifted gracefully away, revealing a handsome, broad-shouldered, whiskered and well-dressed Teddy, smiling like a four-year-old on Christmas morning and blinking tears from his eyes.

"I'm back."

"So, I see," Stella said, smiling with restraint. "You still seem rather far away, from over here."

And with that Stella and Teddy ran to each other and collided in a flurry of affection in the centre of the room. They alternated between holding and kissing one another with all the energy and awkwardness of a love held in the bounds of poverty, youth and deprivation for a lifetime.

"I went to my father's house, where we lived in Jaipur," said Teddy, breaking a kiss long and far enough to speak. "I remembered it, as if from a dream. I saw that fountain…" Teddy gestured with his chin to the picture on the mantelpiece, taken before a tiled fountain in a marbled compound, "…and I had tea with the family living in your house.

I remembered no details, of course, but a feeling. I was close to you there, Stella. Something started in that house, and then that's where it stopped, and stayed suspended in time, until we were brought together again at the orphanage."

"Did you learn what happened?"

"It's a most extraordinary tale," said Teddy with a nod. He released Stella from his embrace and walked to the mantelpiece. "You were kidnapped. It was widely assumed that you'd been killed, particularly when a notorious criminal with some connection to our parents was himself found savagely murdered. Your parents died of sorrow, I understand, and my own father was killed in some disagreement over a contract."

"How did we end up in London? At the same orphanage?"

"That's not entirely clear, but it appears likely that the kidnappers sold you onto the baby market, and you were transported to England. You fell ill during the journey, though, and so you were abandoned at Clerkenwell."

"Which is why I was named Stella Mallory?"

"Yes. The unfortunate one. I was also brought to England, sometime later, by a Christian brother who, by all accounts, had lost his lust for life. When he died I, too, was given over to the orphanage."

"So, we were separated by the gravest of misfortunes, and it was grave misfortune which brought us together."

Teddy smiled at this epiphany.

"I guess that's true," he said. "I remember something you said, many years ago—you never wanted to be lucky, you said. You said that bad luck makes you smarter, stronger. It makes you realise what's important."

"I still believe it. I don't know what would have become of us if I'd never been kidnapped or if we'd never been orphaned or if we'd never been separated, but I know that everything's that happened to us has brought us here, to this moment, with wealth and health and each other."

"I wouldn't have it any other way."

"I remember something you said all those years ago too, Teddy."

"What's that?"

"You said that one day you'd come back to me, and we'd be married."

"I meant it then, and I mean it now. Stella Blythe, will you do me the honour of becoming my wife."

"I will, Teddy Standish," said Stella, "and I consider myself to be the most fortunate girl in the world."

~*~*~

Thank you so much for reading my story.

If you enjoyed reading this book may I suggest that you might also like to read my recent release 'Emma's Forlorn Hope' next which is available on Amazon for just £0.99 or free with Kindle Unlimited.

Click Here to Get Your Copy Today!

Sample of First Chapter

Rain fell hard against the windowpanes, the thick splatters sounding like gunshots in the quiet and dark of the house. Though it was day, the ashen grey clouds blanketed the world like a death shroud. There was a chill in the air, a driving wind clawing its way through the cracks in the stonework and whistling like angered banshees through the house. The raging elements made it hard to think and Emma Moss could not have been more thankful for it. Thinking was the last thing she wanted, as was silence. For the last two days, the house had been quiet as the grave and she could hardly stand it. Angry though the elements were, their raging cacophony was welcome to the nothingness that had taken over her home.

Sat in the rocking chair at her mother's bedside, Emma stared blankly at the windows, watching them rattle whilst trying to count each raindrop. Dark rings circled her eyes and her cheeks were stained with the dried-up channels of tears that no longer flowed. Wrapped in an old, frayed shawl, Emma barely noticed the cold. She was far too numb.

By her side, Emma's mother lay silent and quiet in the bed, covered in as many layers of blankets as Emma could find about the house. She would have had a fire going, except water had gotten to the logs.

She hadn't bothered to complain to Father. Since Mother had fallen ill, the man had come undone. Though never very reliable to begin with, Thomas Moss was nothing without his wife. He was a boat and she the rudder. Emma was told it had always been so, and that her father would never have amounted to anything in life without her mother's influence. Now, as the woman they both loved lay silent and dying in her bed, Emma felt she truly understood the kind of man her father was. Content to wallow in ennui and self-pity, he had holed himself away in the quiet corners of the house for the past days, never once looking to cook for or check after his children. Emma had to ride out to the wet nurse in the nearby village to beg her care for her young sister for a few days, and she was glad she had done so. If left under her father's watch, Emma was certain baby Mary would have been left to starve.

As dissatisfied thoughts of her father swirled through her head, Emma let out a sigh. She tried to ignore the dark and empty fireplace and instead thought about slipping beneath the covers of her mother's bed. Their combined warmth would do them both good, she thought.

With nothing to be done until dinner and the doctor's next visit, Emma made up her mind. Rising up from the chair, the floor creaked loudly underfoot as she moved around the bed and slipped beneath the patchwork covers. She had hoped she was quiet enough not to disturb her mother's rest, but she felt a stirring beneath the sheets as she lay down next to the woman who had raised and nurtured her.

"Thomas… Is that you? Finally risked coming back to your own bed?"

"No, Mama, it's me," Emma spoke softly. She heaved a sigh as she turned her head into the pillows. She wanted to apologise for her father never being there, but it was not her crime to apologise for.

"Your father still sitting in the living room? If he's not careful he'll run out of chances to see me," Mrs Moss said, her voice a pitiful whisper.

"Don't speak like that Mother," Emma said, pushing in a little closer and wrapping her arms around the woman who had raised her.

"Where's Mary?" Mrs Moss asked, before descending into a fit of coughing. Emma sat up and passed over a pewter cup of water. Her mother swallowed a few grateful sips then coughed again.

As Emma took back the glass, she could not help but notice the flecks of blood on the rim of the cup. "Where's Mary?" the woman asked again.

"I told you last time you woke, I sent her to Elsie Brown, the wet nurse. She's promised to look after Mary at no charge until you get better."

"Does she know that'll mean adopting her?" Mrs Moss asked, her gallows humour earning no laugh from her daughter.

The room fell to silence once more, mother and daughter both lying wrapped up together and listening to the sound of the driving rain. Emma held her mother tight in her arms, possessively.

"You know you can't afford to be like your father," Emma heard her mother say, her voice softer.

"Mother?"

"You can't keep going through life finding ways to pretend everything is fine when the house is burning down around you."

"I don't think there is any chance of that with all this rain," Emma joked, trying desperately to deflect her mother's message.

"You know what I mean, Emma," her mother said. She turned now, staring into her eldest daughter's eyes. It was the most alert and together she had seemed in days and yet Emma felt a shudder pass through her as she studied her mother's face. It was so sallow, her skin like paper hanging off her bones. Her hair was limp and lifeless, and she just seemed exhausted—thoroughly and completely. "I want to know that you will look after Mary," the woman continued. There was an edge to her voice, her request one that Emma could not dismiss or bat aside with empty assurances.

"Will you look after Mary when I am gone, Emma?" her mother asked again. Beneath the sheets, her hands moved to find her daughter's, winding their fingers together and grasping tight. "I need to know that you won't abandon her or let anything bad happen to her. I… I love your father, but I know what he is like, too. He won't be any good at all when I'm gone. I need to know I can rely on you to look after yourself and your sister."

Emma bit her bottom lip. She thought she was done with crying. In the last days she had shed so many tears she felt certain she had nothing left to give. Still, as she tried to summon up the words to answer her mother, she felt the familiar dampness on her cheeks, the hateful blurring at the edges of her vision. She couldn't refuse to answer her mother, at the same time she wanted so desperately to ignore the question. Emma couldn't explain it, but she felt at that moment as if she had the power over life and death with her answer. It felt like her mother was asking for her permission to die, ready to slip away once Emma gave her the assurance that she needed to enter that last and deepest of rests.

"Mother, I…"

"Please, Emma," the woman begged again, her dull eyes staring intently at her.

"You know I won't let anything happen to Mary," Emma said at last. The words were halting, broken between half sobs as she nestled into her mother and rested her head in the crook of her neck.

"That's my good girl," came a voice that seemed eerily peaceful and distant. Emma took deep lungfuls of air as she tried to calm herself. No further words passed between them. Emma did not know what else to say, only able to communicate her feelings by the way she held fast to her mother in the dark.

∼

Her eyes flickered open. Outside, the rain had eased to a dull drizzle and the wind calmed to a respectful whisper. It was later than Emma had expected it to be. The bedroom was swathed in darkness and there was no light from under the door frame. The dark clouds of day had drawn into a night, black as pitch, and Emma could hardly even make out her mother's form in the bed. Even without sight, Emma felt something was wrong.

Her mother was still, her body limp in a way that didn't feel like sleep. Emma's hand ran down her mother's arm, moving to her wrist to check for a pulse. For a moment, Emma's whole body tensed, and her lips pursed with worry. Her eyes stared into the dark ahead of her, unfocused and empty as she confirmed her suspicions.

Although there had been weeks to prepare and days to contemplate the possibility of her mother's death,

Emma had put it off. Lying next to the unmoving and silent body, she felt as if she should feel something. She should start to cry again, wrap her arms about her mother and hold her as grief took over. Those felt like the right and natural things to do, but Emma found no compulsion or desire to do either.

Instead, she sat up. Sat up and pulled herself out of bed, taking a moment to light the nearby candle on the bedside table. In the faint illumination, she busied herself. She straightened the bed sheets and turned her mother so that she lay flat on her back with hands clasped together over her chest. This done, Emma found her shoes and slipped them on.

Stepping out into the hall, the girl found no light shining anywhere in the house. She held the candle in her hand firmly as she walked through to the living area and kitchen. There was a weak two-day-old broth in one of the pans left for them to eat. It was not much, but it would do until she could go out to the town in the morning. Finding the last of the coal in the kitchen, Emma set about lighting the stove, making a mental note of all that would need doing the next day.

THE GRAVEST OF MISFORTUNES

There was the undertaker to inform and the parish priest. Doctor Philips would also need to know, and as Emma thought of the man, she wondered why he had not called as agreed. It did not matter much she told herself, focussing on what food she would need to purchase. How long could she leave Mary in the care of Mrs Brown? She had no doubt the kindly wet nurse would agree to look after her baby sister as long as was needed, but Emma couldn't take advantage of that generosity. Besides, she had promised mother that she would see to Mary.

The ongoing list of duties, responsibilities and plans marched on through Emma's mind as she stirred up the old broth in the pan. She stared into the liquid, hardly noticing as a shadow moved behind her. Only when the corner chair creaked did she realise her father had walked in. No doubt he could smell the food.

"How is she?" came the tentative question.

Emma almost didn't want to answer. She wasn't looking to spare her father's feelings or avoid the topic. Instead, she felt as though he had no right to know what had happened. He had chosen to lock himself away the last days and nights, resolutely shuttering the world out to wallow in self-pity. He didn't deserve to know anything. If he wanted to know he should march into his bedroom and see for himself.

"She's dead," Emma answered simply, knowing it would do no good to indulge in petty revenge. She stopped stirring the broth in the pan for a moment, listening for any sign of life or emotion behind her. She did not turn around though, not wishing to look her father in the eyes.

"Was it quick?" The man's voice was weak when he spoke, but Emma heard it.

"I don't know. I know she had fallen asleep. I closed my eyes to rest and when I woke again, she was gone." There was no emotion in her voice, just facts; as if she was telling the news of someone wholly unrelated to her.

For a few minutes, all was silent. Father said nothing, and Emma could not hear him stirring from his chair behind her. She continued with the cooking, stirring the remaining soup until it was bubbling hot. She then dished the meagre meal into two bowls and carried them over to the table. One she lay down before her father, not even looking him in the eyes as she did so. The other, she took to her own place.

"I'll need to see several people in town tomorrow," Emma said, her voice wooden and mechanical. "You'll need to see about going back to work soon. I can't look after Mary and go out to wash and clean for the Parr family."

"We'll move to the city," Thomas said, his voice matter of fact and strangely resolute. He too seemed numbed by everything, left empty and emotionless.

"The city?" Emma sucked in a breath, feeling a twinge of uncertainty. "Why would you say that?"

"It's where the work is," Thomas replied. "I can't expect to get anything here, not after what happened around the time your mother fell ill. Besides, I don't much feel like staying on in this place."

Emma took a sip of soup between pursed lips. "Do you know what you'd do in London?" she asked, trying to put on that voice her mother used to keep a check on him.

"I'll find something," he said, following the words up with a too-casual shrug.

And that was the end of it. Both numb, both unwilling or unable to grieve as they should, father and daughter ate their meal in silence, with the prospect of a new start in the city added to Emma's fears and uncertainties for the future…

~*~*~

This wonderful Victorian Romance story — 'Emma's Forlorn Hope' — is available on Amazon for just £0.99 or *FREE* with Kindle Unlimited simply by clicking on the link below.

[Click Here to Get Your Copy of 'Emma's Forlorn Hope' - Today!](#)

A NOTE FROM THE AUTHOR

Dear Reader,

Thank you so much for choosing and reading my story — I sincerely hope it lived up to your expectations and that you enjoyed it as much as I loved writing about the Victorian era.

This age was a time of great industrial expansion with new inventions and advancements.

However, it is true to say that there was a distinct disparity amongst the population at that time — one that I like to emphasise, allowing the characters in my stories to have the chance to grow and change their lives for the better.

Best Wishes
Ella Cornish

Newsletter

If you love reading Victorian Romance stories…

Simply sign up here and get your FREE copy of The Orphan's Despair

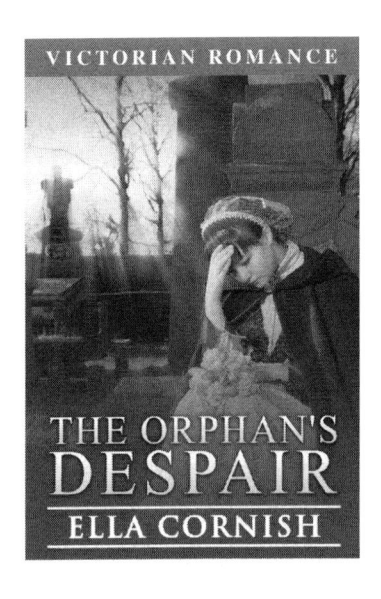

Click Here to Download Your Copy - Today!

∼

More Stories from Ella!

If you enjoyed reading this story you can find more great reads from Ella on Amazon…

Click Here for More Stories from Ella Cornish

∽

Contact Me

If you'd simply like to drop us a line you can contact us at **ellacornishauthor@gmail.com**

You can also connect with me on my Facebook Page **https://www.facebook.com/ellacornishauthor/**

I will always let you know about new releases on my Facebook page, so it is worth liking that if you get the chance.

LIKE Ella's Facebook Page ***HERE***

I welcome your thoughts and would love to hear from you!

Printed in Great Britain
by Amazon